There's a Hearse In My Parking Space

A Church Murder Mystery
Trilogy – Vol. II

By
Thomas L. Shanklin

THERE'S A HEARSE IN MY PARKING SPACE

N-13: 978-1499631135

ISBN-10: 1499631138

© Thomas L. Shanklin 2014

Published by
Thomas L. Shanklin
16114 Pennington Road
Tampa, Florida 33624
mysterywy@gmail.com

DISCLAIMER

This is a work of fiction. Names, characters, businesses, places, events and incidents are either the products of the author's imagination or used in a fictitious manner. Any resemblance to actual persons, living or dead, or actual events is purely coincidental.

Scripture quoted is from the New Revised Standard Version of the Bible.

Portions of the Liturgy come from the 1928 Book of Common Prayer of the Episcopal Church.

A CHURCH MURDER MYSTERY
A TRILOGY

A Soul to Die For
2013

There's a Hearse in My Parking Space
2014

Up From the Grave
2015

In Memory of
The Rev. Alice Hobbs
Friend, Colleague, Mentor, Storyteller, Historian, Theologian, Sister, Mom, Confidant, Preacher, Spiritual Director and so much more.

THERE'S A HEARSE IN MY PARKING SPACE

Loganwood
A Suburb Close to the Inner City of Boston

The story of a large city church
That is somewhere, anywhere, and everywhere.

A Murder
A Mystery
An Allegory

THERE'S A HEARSE IN MY PARKING SPACE

"Nothing is covered up that will not be uncovered, and nothing secret that will not become known. Therefore whatever you have said in the dark will be heard in the light, and what you have whispered behind closed doors will be proclaimed from the housetop." Luke 12:2-3

THERE'S A HEARSE IN MY PARKING SPACE

INTRODUCTION

They call them tall steeple churches. Their steeples reach to the sky. Their roots go down deep. Every city and town has them. They are on the main streets of North American towns. Their architectural styles vary but their presence is the same. Influence. Status. Society. Money. Power. Decline. They are different but the same. Only the names have been changed to protect the innocent and the guilty, those who are responsible for their church's past, present and future. Except for a few, these churches are a dying breed. Time has passed them by.

Members, the pillars of the community who funded these grand schemes in the name of religion, are long gone. Their roots have been transplanted to the local cemeteries, crematoria, suburbs or secular society. They managed to keep their monuments alive and ticking away with some kind of relevance. Sometimes relevance came in the form of having always done it one way or another. Sometimes just not knowing anything else but what was and is, without thinking of what might be or become.

"Change" was a word rarely spoken. To change, meant to spruce up the paint, mow the lawn, or welcome the occasional person that was different. That kind of change made those on the inside feel as if they were doing something in the name of faith and religion while at the same time doing something for their community.

First Church of Loganwood, a tall steeple church, was beginning to have seen better days. It had stood on the same spot along Main Street across from another tall steeple church for nearly two hundred years. Its reason for coming together as a congregation had long been forgotten. Its reason for building such a massive building on the spot had also been lost. All that could be remembered was the day when the five hundred seat sanctuary with two balconies was full and the massive organ was barely loud enough to accompany the enthusiastic singing.

First Church had an unmistakable presence on Main Street but that presence had changed from being a witness of God's love and forgiveness to occupying a piece of prime real estate that could be used in a more meaningful way.

The building of First Church could at one and the same time be noticed or overlooked. It had been reported on more than one occasion that persons looking for First Church could not find it. The church with its two towers and Tiffany stained glass window sits ten feet from the sidewalk. There is nothing on the small patch of grass or sign to indicate that life exists there. The building, so massive in its structure, overwhelms passersby. On more than one occasion persons standing in front of First Church could not find the church. Its imposing presence overshadowed the fact that it was even there.

The church building gave the impression that it was a fortress. It had been designed to impress and preach but it had become, a fortress with closed doors, bitter snickering, back biting and constant criticism of anyone and everything that looked like being on the verge of change and becoming meaningful again.

The tall steeple remained but the influence, no matter how hard the few tried, was gone. No amount of fund raising and creative programming seemed to save what once was nor create what could be. Grasping at straws for meaning and survival, the congregation was beginning to sell off its Tiffany windows. Even that was merely sticking a finger in the dyke that was hemorrhaging meaning, members and money by the minute.

All the meaninglessness and bickering was the least of their troubles. First Church of Loganwood had no inkling what was in store for its present or survival. They could not imagine something as horrific as murder, no less murder that would challenge their very existence.

The frequent scene of a hearse parked in a space out front was the most visible sign that any activity or life existed at First Church, Loganwood.

THERE'S A HEARSE IN MY PARKING SPACE

CHAPTER ONE
THE HOMECOMING

He still had five miles to go. He could see the twin towers of the church off in the distance. His anxiety began to mount, wondering if he had gotten away with all that he had intended to accomplish.

It was a lonely drive. The miles ticked down on the mile markers as he drove the Maine Turnpike toward Loganwood. His anxiety began to rise. The tires of his red pickup truck counted the miles in their familiar thwack, thwack on the concrete pavement. He didn't need the thwack thwack of the tires nor the mile markers alongside the road to remind him of the week he was leaving behind. He also didn't need to be reminded of what he was returning to.

The week in Maine was a relief from the anxiety and stress of keeping the wall up that he had built over many years in the parish ministry. Rev. Brownell, often addressed as "Lee," had spent many years building a wall between him and his parishioners and church hierarchy. He couldn't let anyone know. His call was clear; to preach the Gospel. But his hidden self was also clear. He had built a wall and now as he returned from a week away, the wall needed to go back up.

He counted the miles as he drove. He mentally worked himself back into his pastor role. Before he got into town, he would stop at the last rest area on I-95 South to change into his "go-to-meeting" clothes. He would empty the truck of any signs of his Maine frolic. He'd then be ready for home.

In Lee's Maine life, he's anonymous, or known only to a few. He's the fellow from down country. The flatlander. The man who shows up in his red pickup truck. He's on a mission. Always the same but now the actors, including himself, had changed. One of the reasons for his Maine getaways was gone.

Quentin Patel had been found murdered in front of the altar. Lee didn't know who did it. All he knew was that his trick, his reason for spending time in that god-forsaken town was gone. There would be no more meetings at the pickle park. There would be no more rendezvous at the side of a road. That was all gone.

As he drove along his heart was sad and frightened at the same time. The murderers, he thought, had been caught. But had his secret been found out? He'd made sure that his little times away from the big city parish with the fortress like church building would remain just that, a trip away. Ophelia Pedens had burned up in the fire. That caused a problem for the local sheriff and distracted the community from investigating the murder of Quentin Patel.

He'd read in the paper that there was some conjecture that the fire had been set. But no one could prove anything. Floy Johnson, the owner of the inn had come under suspicion. Some thought that she might have set the fire to collect insurance. The local folks could not believe that scenario. Floy was too upstanding and transparent. The best explanation locals could come up with was that she was a hoarder, spontaneous combustion happened and it was an unfortunate coincidence that Ophelia was staying at the inn when the fire turned her into toast. She had the honor of being the only and last guest to stay in the historic inn. There would be no more guests.

Lee drove along. Mile one. He crossed over into New Hampshire and then down into Massachusetts. The further away he got from that little town in Maine, the closer he got to his big city parish, the more confident he became. His secret was safe. Ophelia couldn't tell that she'd recognized him and his red pickup truck slinking around. She was gone. Quentin was dead. The murderers were headed for jail. Furthermore, they had no inkling of who he was or where he was from. They only knew that Quentin knew their secrets as much as they knew his. At least they thought they knew his secret. And as for that local cop, Chappy Gunnerson, he couldn't punch his way out of a paper sack. And why would he be interested in an anonymous man in a red pickup truck when there was a murder and an arson more interesting to solve?

Lee didn't know that just in case there was a need, Officer Gunnerson had made note of the number plate of the red pickup truck. Massachusetts, RPMREV. Gunnerson thought it was a curious identity. Someday, he thought, he'd check it out just for fun. Gunnerson liked collecting unusual number plates and funny names. One of his favorites was that of an urologist he knew who lived and worked in Vermont. His number plate was RUPPNGOK?

Lee stopped at the local Seven-Eleven for a coffee and the local paper. Down at the bottom of the front page of the Loganwood Gazette he read, "Local Woman Burned Up In Fire In Maine." He pulled into the Blue Hills, a local park, to drink his coffee, to calm down and to rearrange his story before he saw his wife, Eloise, and the people at the church. He wiped the sweat off his brow.

CHAPTER TWO

THE ARRANGEMENTS

Patchy Frost, better known as Pat, was in charge as usual, or at least she thought she was. She had noticed the newspaper headline, "Local Woman Burned Up In Fire In Maine." She had read the article with a macabre kind of interest until she found out that the woman was Ophelia Pedens. Patchy had known Ophelia for many years. They had worked together on all sorts of committees and events at First Church.

Ophelia was the calming influence in everything that Patchy did. Whereas Pat could be seen coming at you from a distance with her big red rose in her hair or pinned to her dress, Ophelia was the demure type who could get lots of things coordinated and done without ruffling feathers. Not so for Pat.

Pat was a know-it-all, do-it-all type of person. You couldn't miss her on Sunday mornings. If she wasn't adjusting the candles on the altar, she was in the warming kitchen telling the fellowship hour volunteers what to do and how to do it. She was one of the pillars of the church, one of those who is often said to be "like concrete. All mixed up and permanently set."

When Pat found out that Ophelia was the woman that had been burned up in the fire in Maine, she saw an opportunity to shine.

"Where's your husband?" asked Pat of Eloise Choate Brownell, Pastor Brownell's wife. Eloise wasn't much interested in Pat or Ophelia. She was in this for the ride, having always wanted to marry a minister.

"How should I know?" Replied Eloise. "I was glad to see him go off somewhere for a week, get him out of my hair. Maybe he'll find himself and come back ready to be a minister and husband."

Pat made a mental note of that comment. She loved to be Rev. Brownell's pet, helper and do-it-all but she also enjoyed an opportunity to criticize him. It wouldn't make her a bit sad if he did himself in. She was always looking for an excuse to inject some kind of controversy on the Staff-Parish Relations committee. Rev. Brownell had nominated her for that committee thinking she would be a good asset and supporter. He was a poor judge of character. He did not know all he needed to know about Ms. Patchy Frost.

"Well, I hope he gets back here soon. Ophelia is dead and I imagine there ought to be some kind of memorial service since she was a prominent and faithful member of our church." Said Pat.

Eloise nodded her head but didn't show much interest in anything to do with Ophelia nor the church. "Whatever." She mumbled.

"I hope your husband," continued Pat, "gets back here sooner than later. Enough of this going off without telling anyone where he's going, how to contact him or when he's returning."

"You're not alone thinking that," replied Eloise as she walked away leaving Pat standing alone in the sanctuary. She whispered to herself, "He goes off all the time and leaves me wondering where he is. He'll show up eventually. Damn inconsiderate."

Pat began to put together some plans for a memorial for Ophelia. It wasn't the first time that Pat took things into her charge. On more than one occasion the local funeral director, noticing that Pat always seemed in the know, had contacted her about the possibility of a funeral or memorial service at the church. Pat, seeing an opportunity to control never hesitated to speak for the pastor even though it was not her place. It got her in trouble with Rev. Brownell. Sometimes it got her in trouble with agencies. She never thought that her behavior might put the church in legal jeopardy. Rev. Brownell told her on more than one occasion, "How dare you speak for me! You have no idea whether I can or cannot do a funeral on that day. It's not your job to be answering for me nor the church regarding such matters."

That didn't stop Patchy from taking charge. She tingled all over with the thought that Ophelia's death was her opportunity. Rev. Brownell was nowhere to be found. Someone had to get the ball rolling. It might as well be her. First things first. Patchy made a list of things to do.

Contact Will Elwell at the local funeral home.
Find out about a date for a memorial service and set it.
Get the major players in order:
    Otty Bourne, the Organist.
    Vida Hood, Otty's wife and cellist
    Marsha Hargrave, the church secretary
    Barbara Nolan, the women's society

"There," thought Patchy, as she twirled the pencil between her fingers. "That will be a good start. I'll contact each of these and tell them what to do. And, since Brownell is missing, I'll just have to do the eulogy myself." Patchy delighted at the thought. She went into action.

CHAPTER THREE

CALLED TO PLAN

If anything good can be said about Patchy, it is that she was an excellent motivator and organizer. She was inappropriate, when it came to time or decision making, but her organizational ability and her passion for the church could not be taken away from her. Unfortunately the passion too often came through as being bossy. If her ego got away with her, her reason for whatever she was doing was more about her than about the church or the good task at hand.

Patchy had good intentions when she first conceived of the idea of a memorial for Ophelia. They had been long-time friends. She knew more about Ophelia than Rev. Brownell or anyone else in the congregation. It made perfect sense to her to take charge.

Within the hour of her conversation with Eloise, Patchy had contacted everyone she needed to work on planning the memorial. They were told to meet that evening at 7pm and to be ready.

They met in the pastor's office even though Rev. Brownell guarded his office privacy. Patchy had talked Marsha Hargrave, the secretary, into unlocking the office and setting up some coffee, decaf of course. Patchy stopped at Dunkin Donuts down the street because only she knew what she liked. No sense taking a chance that someone else would bring just plain donuts.

With the scene set, Patchy waited for the others to arrive. She sat in the pastor's chair. One by one they arrived. Otty Bourne and Vida Hood came together. Marsha Hargrave sat in the background, to observe, take notes and protect the integrity of the pastor's office. Barbara Nolan arrived with all her bluster. She was always on some toot about the death of her daughter seventeen years ago or the fact her husband, Dudley, was off on business again without her.

To round out the planning committee, Patchy had also asked Thomas Dougal, along with Mercedes Haggenmacher and Calista McCann. Dougal, affectionately referred to as Tom, was the ever present doormat of the church. Since neither Mercedes nor Calista drove, he would give them a ride. He gave all the old ladies, and anyone else, a ride. As for Mercedes and Calista, "They wouldn't be much use on the committee" thought Patchy, "but their presence will make it appear that others have been involved. I'll have Marsha print the names of the planners in the bulletin.

Tom, Mercedes and Calista arrived ten minutes late, but Patchy had waited for their arrival.

"Let's get down to business," said Patchy. "Brownell is missing and we've got a beloved church member lying in wait at the local funeral parlor. You've probably heard that Ophelia Pedens died in a fire up in Maine. Will Elwell contacted me from the funeral home. He was looking for Rev. Brownell. I told him he was away and that he couldn't do a memorial for Ophelia but that I would coordinate one."

"Who died and left YOU boss?" said Otty.

Patchy ignored him and went right on with her plans. "Barbara! You need to get the women together and plan a reception after the service. The service will be two days from now. That should give you enough time to organize them. Make sure they have some deviled eggs, finger sandwiches and coffee, decaf preferably."

Barbara, whose mind was more often than not far off ruminating on the day her seventeen year old daughter was killed in a car accident, rose up in her chair as if to attack. Barbara was a good organizer, if her mind was on the task. When she descended into self-pity for her involvement in her daughter's death she would blankly stare or become aggressive.

"I'll take care of it!" yelled Barbara. "And furthermore, like Otty said, Who died and left YOU boss. Who gave you authority to take on the job of the pastor and arrange the church calendar? Who? Couldn't this all wait?"

"Not on your life," replied Patchy. "We've got a dead body lurking down the street at the Elwell Funeral Home and it needs to be dealt with." With that comment, the others lurched into line. Patchy revealed where her heart was, or wasn't at the moment. Barbara sank back down into her depression, sadness and guilt.

"Otty!" said Patchy. "Otty!" she repeated.

"Yes," Otty replied. He had allowed his mind to wander into a place more pleasant than the meeting and the pastor's office. He could hear strains of "Pass Me not O Gentle Savior," hoping that this whole scene would pass him by. Since he was the organist, he was obligated to participate. "Maybe I'll get some extra money for doing this," Otty thought.

"Yes!" replied Otty. "What now?"

Patchy continued. "You know what is appropriate for a memorial service. We don't want anything that alludes to fire or burning! Nor do we need anything that has to do with blood, no "There is a fountain filled with blood." I don't care how much you like those types of hymns, don't!" she shouted. "Ophelia grew up in the rural area of Massachusetts. She loved the old hymns, so drag out "The Lost Chord" and "Beautiful Isle of Somewhere" and anything else you can find. And make sure you don't blast us all with those dreadful loud sounds of that pipe organ."

"Yes mam," replied Otty. It was easier to just go along than to try to make any suggestions as to what was or wasn't appropriate. Vida Hood didn't say anything nor did she offer to play her cello. Her thoughts had wandered off to what she was going to do with Otty later on that night. She'd play his instrument alright!

"Since I knew Ophelia so well," said Patchy, "I'm going to do the eulogy. I can talk about her family and how much she loved this church. And if Rev. Brownell should show up, he can just sit in the audience."

"I don't think that's very nice," said Mercedes Haggenmacher. Mercedes, which by the way means Mercy, was all about mercy and love and peace. She was a kindly little old lady who was somewhat simple. Even though she was simple, she had her morals and upon occasion would speak up for herself and in this case, for Ophelia.

"I don't think that's very nice," repeated Mercedes. "You're taking charge of something that is not your business so you could at least be nice about it."

"Oh shut up!" blurted out Patchy. She immediately knew she had spoken out of turn and out of her real emotions. She apologized to Mercedes.

"I agree with Mercedes," said Calista. "If we are going to do this service without Rev. Brownell, it needs to be all about Ophelia and not about you or us."

"I agree," said Tom Dougal. "It is better to give than to receive," he began to quote scripture. "Be ye doers of the word, and not merely hearers..." (James 1:22)

"Yes, Yes!" replied Patchy with an angry and exasperated look on her face. "We know all about that, Tom. You keep quoting it to us all the time. Let's get over that scripture stuff and get planning this memorial."

It was no use. Patchy was out of control and in control. She was in her glory with the opportunity to play "pastor" and control those around her. She had not thought far enough ahead to think that the best laid plans could come down like a house of cards with the first gust of wind.

With that, Patchy adjourned the meeting. "Get busy!" she ordered.

CHAPTER FOUR

THE ARRIVAL

Rev. Brownell went straight to First Church. He was all suited up in his clergy collar uniform. He had rehearsed what he would say if anyone asked where he had been. He had rebuilt the wall he had let down when he wandered around Maine.

The drive into town was familiar. He could drive it with his eyes closed. This time however, as he turned the corner onto Main Street, his eyes were wider open than at any other time.

There, parked right smack in front of the main door to the church was a hearse. Will Elwell, the local mortician, was standing out front. He looked left and right guarding his precious near-antique hearse, a 1958 Cadillac. It was something he usually did, anything to avoid conversing with the mourners.

Elwell had become a mortician by default. He needed a job when he was a senior at Loganwood High. He saw the advert on the guidance counselor's bulletin board for an assistant at the Bartlett-Green Funeral home. It seemed like an interesting opportunity so he applied. He didn't dare let on that he was curious about the whole process. He wanted to see a dead body. After that first year he was hooked and old Mr. Green, the owner, took a liking to Elwell. Elwell stayed on through college. Mr. Green died. To Elwell's surprise, he inherited the Bartlett-Green Funeral Home on one condition; that he go to mortician school and learn how to embalm and run a funeral home. The inheritance provided the school funds. So, Elwell, even though not very good at dealing with people in crisis, obliged.

From some blocks away, Brownell could see the hearse and Elwell. He tromped on the gas as rage and apprehension mounted. His tires squealed on the pavement. He ran the red light at Main and Western. "Whatever is going on there," he fumed under his breath, "I'll take care of that." He rammed the red pickup truck into the parking space in front of the hearse, barely avoiding the orange parking cones. Slamming it into reverse, he backed up bumper to bumper with the hearse as if he thought Elwell might try to make a quick getaway with or without a body.

Elwell jumped back from the sidewalk onto the square of grass in front of the fortress of First Church.

"What the hell are you doing?" yelled Elwell.

"WHAT THE GOD DAMN DO YOU THINK YOU ARE DOING?" yelled Brownell back at him all the time looking around to see if anyone had heard his outburst?

"I'm here for a funeral, "replied Elwell with a somewhat shaken voice. "And where have you been?"

"None of your damn business where I've been," said Brownell. "I go away for some relief from this damn place and you take over and hold a funeral! Who died and gave you permission?"

"Ophelia Pedens and Patchy Frost." Answered Elwell. "Ophelia Pedens died in a fire up in Maine last week."

Brownell stepped back as if to think for a moment. "What did Elwell know about that fire," he thought. "Ophelia is dead?" he asked. "And Frost, she's dead too?"

"Frost isn't dead! Ophelia is dead!" said Elwell. "Frost got wind of Ophelia's death from the newspaper and she made arrangements for a service once she heard I was in charge of her, ahem," Elwell cleared his throat. He continued. "Once she found out I was in charge of the toast." He laughed.

"Toast?" asked Brownell, as if he didn't already know.

"Yes Toast!" said Elwell. "That's about all that was left of her. They shipped her down by train two days ago. It'll be

THERE'S A HEARSE IN MY PARKING SPACE

a closed casket because who other than Ms. Frost, wants to see burned meat." He laughed again.

Brownell didn't think it was funny. As he stood there thinking what to do next he thought, "Do they know who set the fire that killed Ophelia? Do they know that I was right there when the fire happened? Do they know why I was in the same town where Ophelia happened to be?" It made him nervous to think that his secret that had turned into multiple secrets, might have been found out.

"Poor Ophelia," said Brownell. "She was such a lovely person and so dedicated to this church. It was all she really had, that and her career. She had no relatives. Patchy was her closest life-long friend."

"Patchy," said Elwell. "She's inside finalizing the arrangements. Since you weren't able to be found, she took over."

"Poor Ophelia," repeated Brownell. "Bossy and inappropriate Patchy, typical of her." His gut began to boil with anger. "How dare her," he thought.

Elwell could sense the conversation was going downhill fast so he stepped back lest Brownell took a swing at him. "I'm just here to help," he said in a timid tone.

"Help. HELP!" shouted Brownell. "And of course make as much money as you can out of this tragedy." Brownell might have been talking about himself as much as about Elwell. On more than one occasion Brownell let slip his true feelings saying "There's money in the ministry." He was often no more interested in providing a pastoral service than other than to get an honorarium and the honorarium better be bigger than what the organist was paid.

Elwell stepped further back from Brownell. The further away he was from Brownell's physical presence and earshot, the better. He didn't trust him. The feeling was mutual.

"I'm here now!" shouted Brownell. "If Frost thinks she's going to act like the pastor and make decisions that involve me and my schedule, she's got another think coming. I'm the pastor here. I'm in charge. I'll do all the services here. Yours is to do what I tell you to do, not what Frost tells you to do. When's the service? How much of the arrangements are made?"

"One o'clock. Two hours from now," replied Elwell. "Frost is in charge. She's coordinated it all."

"We'll see about that!" yelled Brownell as he stormed up the steps into the church.

Elwell was left shaking his head. It wasn't often that he got yelled at. Most, especially grieving survivors, treated him with respect and dignity. Most clergy were cooperative and helpful. "This Brownell guy," he thought, "He's a piece of work. It's a wonder he keeps his job. Someday…" his thoughts trailed off.

CHAPTER FIVE

THE CONFRONTATION

He was barely through the front door of the church when he began yelling.

"WHERE IS SHE!?" Brownell screamed at Mercedes Haggenmacher who was folding bulletins for the service. Mercedes lowered her head as if she'd done something wrong.

"Where's who?" she nervously asked. "And you could say hello before you started yelling." It was one of the few times that Mercedes, usually referred to by her nickname Mercy, spoke up for herself. "Where's who?" she repeated.

"That Patchy Frost," said Brownell as he lowered his volume a notch. "Where is she?"

"She's back in the kitchen helping the ladies with the refreshments," replied Mercy.

"Probably more like telling them what to do, I'd say," retorted Brownell.

Mercy thought about that one a moment before she spoke. Brownell was already half way down the aisle, having gotten what he wanted out of Mercy.

"Welcome back," said Mercy. "And while you're at it, calm down and take care of business with a dose of love for a change," she offered under her breath.

Brownell didn't hear her advice. He was more intent on Patchy Frost and bringing her in line. "How dare she make decisions that are mine to make," he seethed through his teeth under his breath. "I'll take care of her." He slammed the door behind him as he left the sanctuary.

He didn't have far to go. The antiquated kitchen was just a short distance down a hall. He never got there. Patchy had finished telling the ladies what to do and she was headed to the sanctuary. Brownell just about ran her over in his haste to get to her.

He didn't bother to say hello. "Just who do you think you are?" he yelled. "I'm the pastor here. How dare you make decisions in my name! You have no.."

Patchy stopped him in his speech. She was not as demure, nor as tactful, as Mercy.

"Don't yell at me!" she shouted. "You weren't here and someone had to make a decision about Ophelia. We can't have her hanging around day after day. For all I know she might be starting to smell already."

Patchy had a heart of gold, a will of steel, and a take charge personality with a bit of macabre thrown in. Many wondered what side of her was going to come out. She'd been known to tell an off color joke or two, especially when it came to funerals and dead bodies.

"Well, I haven't died, or given up my authority yet. I'm getting pretty damn tired of you making decisions that you have no right to make. You've gotten us into trouble more than once. That time you took money out of my discretionary fund and gave it to an underage girl to get a bus ticket so she could skip town, was just about the last straw. I had to do some fancy footwork with the parents, the women's shelter and their lawyer. And now you make arrangements for a funeral!" He yelled.

"You were nowhere to be found," Patchy offered in her defense. "If you'd tell us where you are and how to get in touch with you, this kind of thing wouldn't happen."

"None of your business where I went, just like your making decisions about my schedule, time, job, is none of your business. I'll take care of this funeral now. You're done! DONE! Get it Patchy? DONE!" he yelled at her as he started to head back to the sanctuary to get a bulletin and prepare to officiate at a funeral.

Calista McCann, Barbara Nolan, Kallie Jansink and Esther Howlane all had been diligently following Patchy's orders in the kitchen. When they heard the commotion going on in the hall, they cracked the door wide enough to hear but not wide enough to be noticed. They took note of the situation. They were stunned by the yelling. They heard this kind of thing happened on more than one occasion. This was the first time they heard it firsthand.

CHAPTER SIX

A MAINE INVESTIGATION

The murder of Quentin Patel in Somewhere might have been easily solved when Gregg Morrison, his mother Merti, and Gloriana Wickware had all confessed. Quentin knew their secrets and their sordid lives. They thought they knew Quentin's secret. They did, but not completely.

Chappy Gunnerson, the local officer, was pleased that he was able to solve the murder in such an efficient way. He didn't have much experience in murder investigation. He had lots of experience in dealing with people of ill repute wherever they were from. In fact, Chappy had little respect for the people in somewhere and a great deal of respect for integrity and the law.

The one inconsistency that seemed to be left unsolved was the fact that Ophelia Pedens had burned up in the Inn. He had come to the conclusion that the Inn owner, Floy Johnson, was innocent. She seemed more to be the victim of the fire than an arsonist. She had lost all her possessions, home and business.

He couldn't quite put the fire mystery out of his mind. For that reason, Chappy kept an "Inn Fire" notepad on the seat of the police cruiser for those times when a clue might appear, or an inspiration might lead to a solution. It was just one of those times that Chappy noticed one to many times the red pickup truck that kept driving around Somewhere. He made a note of the license plate. RPMREV, Massachusetts.

With all the local clues exhausted, with all the local people dismissed as possible suspects, Chappy remembered the red pickup truck. He did a number plate search. The information quickly appeared on the screen of his laptop. It made him even more curious and suspicious.

"RPMREV" – registered to a Rev. Lee Brownell of Loganwood Massachusetts.

Chappy searched a little further in police records for a Lee Brownell. He found a number of reports but none for THE Rev. Lee Brownell. "Humph," mused Chappy, "The man has no record. Not even a traffic citation. But what was he doing in Somewhere the week of the murder and the fire?"

Chappy did a little local investigation. No one, except Gregg Morrison who had gotten off as an accomplice to the murder, even remembered the red pickup truck.

Gregg was the lucky one in the bunch of conspirators. His fabulous steeple sitting, naked body board fantasy, was found to be rather curious by Judge Fairbanks. Fairbanks found it even more enticing when Gregg confessed to spending a great deal of time at the pickle park in a red dress and red stilettos. Gregg was not adverse to soliciting sexual favors. Rumor had it that Fairbanks was not above taking some defendants into his chambers and soliciting sexual favors from them. Chappy couldn't be sure if that was what happened in the Quentin Patel murder case, but Gregg Morrison did get off with just probation for his fringe involvement in the murder. He hadn't carried out the murder but he had encouraged it. He had gone along with it. He had helped with the cover-up.

Gregg Morrison was sentenced to a year house arrest with ten years of probation.

Chappy thought it was worth a try to pay this odd 40ish man a visit at his secluded home up in the woods. "What was he doing now?" thought Chappy. "And," he continued, "What now might he be willing to tell?"

CHAPTER SEVEN

THE BACKWOODS VISIT

Officer Gunnerson drove the five miles out of the village, up the frost heaved and pot-holed back road to Gregg's house. Gregg's truck was in the driveway. He was home.

Gunnerson got out of the cruiser and went to the door. He knocked. He could hear footsteps on the other side. "Why would anyone live out here in this god-forsaken place," he thought.

Just then the door opened wide. There stood Gregg Morrison, naked as a pervert on a body board.

"Put some clothes on!" ordered Gunnerson. "Cover up that little winky. That's nothing to be proud of."

"It's my home and I'll do what I want!" said Gregg. "You could have given fair warning that you were coming. I didn't hear the alarm on the drive go off. Damn thing must have a dead battery again."

"Put some clothes on!" ordered Gunnerson. "I'm not here to encourage your lewd and imbecilic behavior. I've got important business to discuss."

Gregg demurred. He reached for his boxer shorts which satisfied Gunnerson but disappointed Gregg. Gregg was always ready for some encounter that might lead to even stranger behavior than the naked body board love affair.

"You could have called," Gregg repeated himself. "And besides, there is a big sign a few feet up the drive way that reads. 'CAUTION. BEYOND THIS POINT YOU MAY ENCOUTER NUDISM. ENTER AT YOUR OWN RISK."

"Yeah, Yeah,"replied Gunnerson with an irritated tone.

"I need to talk with you, so may I come in or are we going to stand here, face to boxer shorts?"

"Sure. Come in," invited Gregg. "Have a seat. How about a coffee, or maybe a shot of whiskey."

"Not on your life!" said Gunnerson. "You've already gotten your life into a nice pickle, I'm not going to ruin mine. Now, tell me, did you happen to notice a man driving a red pickup truck the week Quentin Patel was murdered?"

Gregg thought for a while.

"Well, did you?" continued Gunnerson.

"I'm thinking," replied Gregg. "Am I going to get into any more trouble? I'm happy to be confined to this house and these woods. I can do as I like here, be as naked as much as I want."

"Yeah, yeah,"countered Gunnerson. "Answer the question. Do you remember seeing a man driving around in a red pickup truck?"

"Yes," said Gregg.

"And? Continue."

"Yes," repeated Gregg."I'm not in trouble again, am I?"

"No. Just answer the question."

"Okay then," continued Gregg. "I did notice a red pickup truck. I've seen him around here before. Every so often he would appear. I most often saw him,"

"You most often saw him where? When," interrupted Gunnerson.

"I most often saw him…" Gregg hesitated. "This won't get me in trouble will it?"

"No." answered Gunnerson. "I just want to know what you know about this guy in the red pickup."

"Okay." Continued Gregg. "I usually saw him down at the pickle park. That's where I discovered Quentin Patel's secret rendezvous he would have. Red pickup truck man would arrive close to dark every so often. Quentin would arrive shortly thereafter. When they thought no one was watching, they would disappear into the woods for..."

"For?" asked Gunnerson.

"For," Gregg hesitated.

"For? Go on..."

Gregg continued, "For the same reason I or anyone stops at a secluded spot close to dark. To do whatever one does in the dark, out of sight from others."

"What does that mean?" said Gunnerson.

"Well," Gregg continued. Gregg was now getting excited himself to be able to reveal once again one of his secret places and his secret activities. "I go there to hang out in my red dress and..."

"And what?"

"And sometimes other interesting things happen." Gregg said with a chuckle.

"Stop being mysterious. You're enjoying this way too much," said Gunnerson. "And what?"

"Like Gloriana tending to her pot growing field. Like people doing private things in the woods. Like..."

"Okay, I get it," interrupted Gunnerson. "Sexual favors or other illicit or borderline illicit activities that one doesn't want to get caught doing but which one can't stop themselves from doing."

"What's this all about?" asked Gregg.

"The fire at the Inn." Said Gunnerson. "It's never been solved. I have an inkling that there's more to this whole fire story. I think it was murder. The woman burned in the fire was the one who discovered the murdered Quentin. You knew that. But at the time only Floy Johnson knew that. There seems to be some reason for the fire other than a run down, fire trap of a building and spontaneous combustion."

"Interesting," said Gregg as he adjusted himself in his boxer shorts. "Exciting too."

"Stop doing that!" said Gunnerson. "I hope you're done with pickle park visits. You've been helpful."

"Really? "said Gregg with a squirrely grin. "Really? How so? Who is that man anyway?"

"A minister who I suspect," answered Gunnerson, "was in these parts for some less than honorable reason. I made a note of his license plate number just in case. It appears that he and Ophelia were from the same area of Massachusetts."

"Where?" said Gregg.

"Loganwood," replied Gunnerson as he got up and headed to the police cruiser.

"Loganwood," whispered Gregg. "Come again anytime," he shouted as Gunnerson roared off.

"Loganwood."

CHAPTER EIGHT

THE FUNERAL

*"There is a way that seems right to a person,
but its end is the way of death."
Proverbs 14:12*

It was Tuesday. Rev. Brownell especially liked funerals that were scheduled for Tuesdays. It gave him a chance to recover from the rigorous schedule on Sunday that he kept each week. This week was different, however. He took two days to drive down from Maine, arriving on Tuesday. He arrived just in time to stop Patchy Frost from carrying out her plan for Ophelia's funeral. He would be in charge, not Patchy.

Will Elwell had gotten over his sidewalk encounter with Brownell. He was back to his usual funereal personality. He was more of a "stand around and be quiet organizer guy" than "chitty chatty." Mourners were starting to arrive for the 1pm funeral so he had to engage in some conversation. Small talk.

"Hello Mr. Elwell. So sorry about Ophelia."

"Nice to see you, Mr. Elwell. I so appreciated your assistance with Mom's funeral.

"Beautiful day, Mr. Elwell."

Nothing conversations. That suited Will Elwell just fine. He preferred it that way. The important conversations had already happened at the funeral home where he was in his element. There he went into his grand sales pitch leading up to some exorbitant fees as he preyed upon the grief of survivors. In the case of Ophelia, there were no survivors, except for her friend Patchy and as regards Patchy, the further away he got from her the better.

"Give me the nod when it's time to begin," said Brownell as he approached Elwell in the back of the sanctuary. Brownell was in his white robe and ready to go. The service Patchy had put together, thankfully, was the standard one. The only thing different was some of the unusual music. He could deal with the fact that Patchy's name was listed at the point of the Eulogy. He'd just ignore it and say what he had to say about Ophelia.

"Before we begin," said Brownell, "I need to chat with the organist."

Otty Bourne had arrived early and was already seated at the big pipe organ console. He was doodling on the organ. He was playing a sort of meek, mild and meaningless type of traveling music. He knew the usual funeral hymns. They always made him think of the Titanic sinking to the tune of "Nearer My God to Thee." He often wondered just how near those poor freezing and departed souls were as they heard that tune. The same applied to any deceased he played a funeral for.

"Otty," said Brownell. "We need to chat for a moment."

Otty continued his doodling. People continued to file into their seats. Otty nodded.

"These hymns," said Brownell, "that Patchy picked. I know some of them are Ophelia's favorites. That's fine. But, Please, please," he pleaded, "Please let's not play them as if we are at a funeral."

Otty looked up with one of his usual, "Damn You" grins. He'd heard that speech before and he'd damn well do what he wanted. "I'm in charge of the beast of an instrument and I can make more noise than you," he thought to himself. Otty nodded in agreement while all the time determined to play as he pleased.

"One of Ophelia's favorite organ pieces," said Otty, "was The Lost Chord. I have wished more than once that it had never been written. But nevertheless, it was and she liked it. So before you start, I'm playing it as a prelude."

"I hate it too, "said Brownell, "but let's just get this thing over with and the toast of a body in the ground." He walked away to leave Otty to his devices. Sometimes he was successful at demanding Otty play a certain way, other times he was not. He suspected today was not going to be a good day.

Will Elwell got Brownell's attention. "Psst!" he signaled. "Tell the organist to begin and you follow the prelude with the service."

"I know what I'm doing!" replied Brownell as if he had just experienced the insult of the century. "And Otty knows what to play. Give him the signal."

Elwell gave a wave of the hand that Otty saw in his organ rear-view mirror. The strains of The Lost Chord started to come out of the organ pipes like black smoke out of the papal chimney when another vote had been taken and no pope was elected.

Some old timers began to hum along. Some even knew the words to that old sawhorse of a Victorian song.

THE LOST CHORD
Music by Sir Arthur Sullivan;
Words by Adelaide Anne Proctor

Seated one day at the organ, I was weary and ill at ease,
And my fingers wander'd idly over the noisy keys;

I knew not what I was playing, or what I was dreaming then,
But I struck one chord of music like the sound of a great Amen.

It flooded the crimson twilight like the close of an Angel's Psalm,
And it lay on my fever'd spirit with a touch of infinite calm.

It quieted pain and sorrow like love overcoming strife,

It seem'd the harmonious echo from our discordant life.

*It link'd all perplexed meanings into one perfect peace
And trembled away into silence as if it were loth to cease;*

*I have sought, but I seek it vainly, that one lost chord divine,
Which came from the soul of the organ and enter'd into mine.*

*It may be that Death's bright Angel will speak in that chord again;
It may be that only in Heav'n I shall hear that grand Amen!*

By the time Otty had found and played the "lost chord," Rev. Brownell had made his way to the platform. He'd put on his most ministerial and funereal face and demeanor. He began.

"Dearly beloved, we are gathered here in the sight of God and these witnesses to unite..." Just then he caught himself. Several people in the congregation gasped and whispered to each other, "He's reading the service for a wedding!" Brownell started over.

I am the resurrection and the life, saith the Lord; he that believeth in me, though he were dead, yet shall he live; and whosoever liveth and believeth in me shall never die. Blessed are the dead who die in the Lord; even so saith the Spirit, for they rest from their labors. Today we are gathered to celebrate the life and death of our beloved sister, Ophelia Pedens.

Officer Gunnerson watched from the last row of the sanctuary. Brownell could hear some people crying. He watched them daub at tears. Patchy Frost sat front and center with her arms crossed and a scowl on her face. Brownell had taken away the opportunity for her to shine!

The congregation wasn't much for singing. Brownell was thankful that Patchy had put in only one hymn for them to sing. The rest of the music was either by organ or a soloist. Unfortunately the soloist was Veona Rotowitz. She had seen better days, at least her voice had. Brownell thought, "What's worse; this congregation trembling through a hymn or Rotorooter warbling off key." He didn't have to choose. Patchy had chosen for him and it was Veona. It was her time.

Veona went and stood by the big organ console. She nodded and Otty, prepared for off key singing and screechy old lady high notes, began. The song Patchy had chosen was "Beautiful Isle of Somewhere," written by Jesse B. Pounds for the funeral of President McKinley after he was murdered. And since it was entirely possible that Ophelia was murdered and lay in front of them, toast in a box, the song was quite appropriate.

Veona began.

Somewhere the sun is shining,
Somewhere the songbirds dwell;
Hush, then, thy sad repining,
God lives, and all is well.

Refrain

Somewhere, somewhere,
Beautiful Isle of Somewhere!
Land of the true, where we live anew,
Beautiful Isle of Somewhere!

Somewhere the day is longer,
Somewhere the task is done;
Somewhere the heart is stronger,
Somewhere the guerdon won.

Somewhere the load is lifted,
Close by an open door;
Somewhere the clouds are rifted,
Somewhere the angels sing.

"Well, she managed to get through that without too much screeching," thought Brownell. "I wonder what toast looks like after being burned up in a fire." He shuddered at the thought of Ophelia, all black and charred, lying there dead as an ash in that cheap grey cloth covered casket. "They should have put a pall over that ugly casket, or at least Patchy could have picked a cheap metal one. Ophelia liked blue." His mind wandered but came back to the presence in the room when Veona hit the final off key high note.

Gunnerson cringed. He also wondered what Ophelia now looked like in that grey box. Had they even tried to do anything to her? Many in the congregation were dozing off or in their minds, visiting former funerals. Some were even pondering their own funerals. Many knew they did not want Rev. Brownell officiating at theirs. Too often he told lies about the deceased. They sat in anticipation of what he might say about Ophelia. They also sat there somewhat perplexed that he was nowhere to be found when she died and arrived back in Loganwood.

Otty doodled on the organ, using the melody from "Beautiful Isle" while he waited for Brownell to gather his thoughts back into the present. Brownell stepped to the pulpit. Otty announced the end of the quiet and Brownell's arrival to speak with a grand "Beautiful Isle of Somewhere" fanfare! Brownell looked over with disapproving eyes, but what could he do, Otty was in charge of an instrument much bigger than his. Bigger. Louder. More effective at getting the attention of a congregation.

Brownell led the congregation in reciting the Twenty Third Psalm and asking them to stand, he read the familiar resurrection scriptures from the gospels.

"I am the resurrection and the life," he intoned. "He who believes in me shall never die." He asked the congregation to be seated all along as he thought, "What drivel. Does anyone believe in this stuff?"

Patchy looked more furious than ever because now was the point in the service where she would have puffed herself up and made everyone oooh and aaah over the words she was about to speak about Ophelia.

Officer Gunnerson sat up straight. This was the point in the service he was waiting for. He wanted to hear what people had to say about Ophelia and, if possible, would someone implicate themselves. Was Ophelia murdered or was the fire just a coincidence?

Rev. Brownell, in his most ministerial and solemn voice began. He told of Ophelia having been born and raised in Loganwood. He spoke of her early years, none of which he knew. He told of her kindness and integrity both in the workplace and as a member of First Church. Best of all, he told of how much he loved and respected her. These were words that were not worth hearing nor writing down.

Officer Gunnerson wondered about what he was hearing. Patchy silently "harrumphed her way through the eulogy all the time thinking, "What a pack of lies. He didn't really know her. He never gave her the time of day. I knew her better than anyone here. I should be speaking for Ophelia, not Brownell."

Will Elwell and Brownell had decided that since Ophelia had so few relatives, there was no point dragging a whole congregation out to the cemetery for a committal and burial. So with the closing strains of "When the Roll is Called Up Yonder," Rev. Brownell went right into the words that are often spoken at the cemetery.

He was glad to wrap it up in the sanctuary than at the cemetery. First off, he always got stuck hanging around the grave longer than he wanted. Last time he did a burial out at Eveningtide Cemetery was in the dead of winter. He had gotten his red pickup truck stuck on a pile of ice. He had gone to the wrong grave and had to walk in two feet of snow across half the cemetery to the correct grave. In the process he had fallen down in the snow and was the laughing stock of those waiting with the body at the correct grave. Finally, the grave diggers had to get his pickup unstuck from the ice so he could go home. So Brownell was very happy to be done with Ophelia in the sanctuary so he could get on with whatever getting on he was up to.

"Ashes to Ashes, dust to dust" he intoned. "We commit this body to the ground." Thankfully, once again, he had not repeated the little ditty a friend had told him years before. "Ashes to ashes dust to dust, if you didn't have an asshole your belly would bust." He chuckled inside as he spoke the correct words, and with a grand "AMEN" he was down the aisle, out in his red pickup truck and free of a congregation that couldn't care less about him or about their church business.

Gunnerson watched in stunned silence.

CHAPTER NINE

FOOD FOR THOUGHT

Officer Gunnerson watched the congregation as Patchy Frost invited them to all gather in fellowship hall for some refreshments and conversation. Gunnerson joined them even though he was from Maine and had nothing to do, other than curiosity, with these people.

He stood off in a corner watching the people relate to each other and deciding with whom he would like to speak.

Otty Bourne, the organist, was the first to approach him and offer a word of greeting. "Hello, sir," said Otty. "Are you from here? I notice you're in uniform and wondered."

"No," replied Gunnerson. "I'm from Somewhere in Maine. That's where Ms. Pedens died in the fire. I'm curious about her. Why was she in Maine? Why did she die in the fire?"

"I've wondered that too," replied Otty. "Ophelia loved to travel and I suspect she was just away on one of her weekend jaunts. I was sad to hear she had burned up. She was a good woman. She couldn't hurt a flea. She was a big supporter of this church. She especially liked my playing."

"That's interesting." Said Gunnerson. "What did you think of Rev. Brownell's eulogy? Was he accurate in what he had to say about Ophelia? It sounded like he knew her very well."

Otty hesitated. He always had a hard time not telling the truth. Should he keep mum and not tell the truth or tell the truth and perhaps put himself and others in jeopardy. He decided to tell the truth. "Rev. Brownell," he began, "barely knew Ophelia. He used her when he needed something done. He took her money. He often asked her for big donations because he knew she'd received an inheritance plus she'd saved for many years. The sad thing is, she was so willing to give but he was so unwilling to return the favor."

"How do you mean?" Said Gunnerson.

"Can I be honest with you?" Said Otty?

"Please," encouraged Gunnerson.

"Brownell," continued Otty, "In my opinion is just in this for the money and glory. He doesn't go out of his way for anyone unless he wants something. He doesn't allow anyone to use their gifts for the love and ministry of this church. And, worst of all, he's a user."

"What do you mean, User?" asked Gunnerson.

"He gets what he wants out of people," said Otty, "and then when he's done, he's done with them. That eulogy he just spoke this afternoon.."

"Yes," interrupted Gunnerson

"That eulogy," said Otty, "was nice, but it was more about Brownell than Ophelia. He had no clue what Ophelia was really like. He made up a pack of lies. No one who heard it will confront him with the truth. He gets away with murder most of the time. Did you notice how fast he left after the service?"

"I did. I would have liked to have spoken with him but he was gone in a flash." Said Gunnerson. "What do you suppose that was all about?"

"He hates coffee hours," said Otty, "And anything to do with socializing with the congregation. He does as little as possible while giving the impression that he is constantly on their side and doing for them. And, all in the name of God. It's sick."

"And this woman, Patchy Frost?" Said Gunnerson. "What about her?"

"That's her over there." Said Otty. "The one with the big red flower in her hair and the fancy look-at-me dress. She's a good person, but she can be mighty aggressive and in your face too. She butts heads with Brownell all the time. Most of the people just take her for who she is and go along with her eccentricity, smelly perfume and demanding orders."

"Excuse me," said Otty. "Tomorrow is our Wednesday night choir rehearsal and I need to speak with some of my choir members before they leave. We're getting ready with some special music and I need to be sure to encourage them to rehearse."

"Well, thank you," said Gunnerson. "It's been nice to meet and chat with you. You've been very helpful. Perhaps we'll have another opportunity to chat. I think I have no need to speak with anyone else here right now. Perhaps I'll pay a visit to Chief Jane Blanc. It is common courtesy to let a town's Police Chief know when another is in town doing an investigation. You have a nice afternoon."

"It was nice to meet you. I wish you all the best" said Otty as the two parted. Otty headed toward the little gaggle of choir members conflab in the corner. Gunnerson headed for his cruiser and the local Police station.

CHAPTER TEN

A COURTESY CALL

It wasn't difficult for Officer Gunnerson to find the Loganwood Police Station. It was right next to the town hall a few blocks west of First Church. He parked the cruiser in the visitor spot and found the door opening into a lobby with a dispatcher sitting behind a glass.

"May I help you?" asked the dispatcher.

"Yes," replied Gunnerson. "I'm officer Gunnerson from Somewhere, Maine. I'd like to speak with the Chief of Police. Can you tell me his name?"

"Her name is Jane Blanc," replied the dispatcher. "I'll see if she is available. Please have a seat while I check."

The dispatcher returned shortly and indicated that Chief Blanc would be out.

The door to the inner sanctum of the police station opened and it was the Chief.

"Good afternoon, Officer Gunnerson, I'm Chief Blanc," she said. "Your name sounds familiar. Come in to my office."

Gunnerson followed her down a hall to the chief's office where he was offered a chair across from her desk.

"How may I help you?" said Chief Blanc.

"Well, I'm in town doing a little investigating about an incident that happened in my town, Somewhere Maine. I suspect we might have a murder on our hands and there's a possibility that it might have some connection to Loganwood. You may have read about a fire in your local paper." He offered.

"When did the fire happen?" She asked.

"It happened about two weeks ago. I understand there was an article in the Loganwood Gazette telling of a Ms.

Ophelia Pedens dying in a fire in an Inn in Somewhere. Did you happen to read that?" he asked.

"Yes. I remember seeing that headline but I didn't read the entire article. I have all to do to keep up with the law breakers here in Loganwood." She commented. "Why do you think there might be something to be learned here about a fire and a murder?"

"Ophelia Pedens," he replied, "was the person who discovered the murdered body of Quentin Patel in our little local church. The murder led to the demise of the church and the congregation. Three people in the congregation had conspired to murder him. They knew his secrets and he knew theirs so they did him in. Ophelia discovered the body and reported it to me. I had met with her a number of times and even asked her to stay in town at the Inn for a day or two while I did some investigating. It was during that time the Inn caught fire and Ophelia burned up in it. There was no reason for the fire it seemed and there was no reason to think anything about Loganwood other than this is where she came from, until I did a license plate check on a red pickup that was hanging around Somewhere at the same time that Ophelia was there."

"I see," said the chief. The story was sparking her interest. "And what did you find out?"

"The red pickup truck belongs to a Rev. Brownell who lives here in Loganwood and is pastor at First Church. I just came from Ophelia's funeral at First Church. Rev. Brownell officiated. It was an interesting funeral. I had a conversation with the organist, Otty Bourne, about the whole scene, Ophelia, Brownell, and the funeral." Said Gunnerson.

"What did you find out?" asked Chief Brace.

"A number of things," he replied. "That Brownell didn't really know Ophelia very well. That Brownell didn't just happen to be in Somewhere the same time Ophelia was there, he made regular trips there for less than honorable reasons. That Brownell has a strangle hold on that congregation and often disappears without notice. That .."

Chief Brace interrupted him. "How can I help? It appears that you have a lot of suspicion going on but a lot of it is circumstantial evidence. Do you have anything concrete besides the fact that they were both in your town in Maine at the same time?"

"Nothing other than Brownell seems to be living a double life." Gunnerson concluded. "One here in Loganwood, a professional life and one in Somewhere, a life of sexual fantasy and slinking around. Do you know anything more that might be helpful?"

"Nothing very earth shattering." She replied. "He's been in town for some years. He has no children. His wife is involved in lots of community affairs but I hear that they don't have much of a home life. I suspect she's in it for the money, as much as it often appears he is. There are rumors going around town that their marriage is more one of convenience than love. And the church appears to be on the decline. Don't' get me wrong, he does have the respect of some in town but many have left and gone across the street to the White Church. I've even heard reports of one or two people parking in First Church's parking lot, walking in the back door, picking up Sunday's bulletin and then walking out the front door and going across the street to White Church."

"Amazing," replied Gunnerson. "But that probably doesn't have anything to do with murder. Probably has more to do with how he does or doesn't relate to his people. Well, thank you for your assistance. I'd appreciate it if you would call me if you can think of anything or hear anything. I'll hang around here a few more days and probably have some more conversations with some locals. Maybe just hang out in civilian clothes and listen to conversations at the local Dunkin Donuts or First Morning Brunchies."

"Good idea," said the Chief. "Let me know if I can be of any help. Nice to meet you."

SUNDAY MORNING
Following Ophelia's Funeral
On the previous Tuesday

CHAPTER TWELVE

THE DISCOVERY

Otty Bourne was always early on Sunday mornings. He had lots of music to prepare for the morning worship and he didn't want to get side-tracked by some well-meaning soul. Mercedes Haggenmacher was often there early. If he could get there before her, he would have a chance to shuffle his music, set the organ stops and relax a bit before the choir showed up.

The service was at 10:30. Otty arrived at 9:30. Mercedes got there at 9:45 am and busied herself folding bulletins and making sure that the hymnals were properly arranged in the pews.

Rev. Brownell was already in his office. That wasn't so unusual because he often waited until Sunday morning to write, finish, or polish up his sermon. He appreciated the quiet of the church and the aloneness with the manuscript and, although he wouldn't admit it, God.

There was no reason for any of the three to disturb each other. Each went about their business.

Otty spent some time arranging the music into proper order for the morning worship. That made it easier than to hunt through hymnals and stacks of music for what came next in the order of worship. When he had it all arranged, he then practiced. That was no different than any other Sunday, or from Ophelia's funeral a few days before, for that matter.

Otty sat down at the big four manual console of the pipe organ. It was the pride and joy of the congregation. The Osterhouser family had donated the bulk of the money back in the 1920's to purchase the instrument. It was the largest one in town and that was important because the big churches on Main Street not only were engaged in ministry in the name of Jesus, they were also enmeshed in a battle. They battled for the elite of the town. They battled for money. They battled for the best programs. And they battled over who had the best pipe organ and organist.

As far as Otty was concerned, he was the best organist in town, a graduate of Eastman School of Music. And he was master of the best organ in town with over 50 ranks of pipes and a myriad of sounds ranging from the smallest pencil thin flue or flute pipes, to the biggest of big, 64 foot bombards. The organ was massive to look at. It was impressive to hear. It was a joy to play when everything was in proper working order. It usually was.

Otty flicked the switch that activated the big orgel-blow, the blower in the basement. He could hear the wind rushing up through the ductwork into the air chambers. A wheeze here and there was nothing. It was just an indication that the air was doing what it was supposed to do. Each time the organ was turned on, the air would fill the wind chests to capacity and then settle down to wait for the organist to activate a stop here or there and begin to make music from the massive keyboards.

The organ was ready. Otty was ready. He opened his Widor-Schweizter edition of the Works of Bach to the Toccata and Fugue in D Minor. Everyone knew that piece. They often associated the Toccata with Halloween and macabre scenes. Since Halloween was past he had decided to play only the fugue as a prelude.

He pulled the stops that would make the sound that would make the music. Principal chorus was always a good choice on the Great Manual: Principle 8', 4', 2' and a four rank mixture. Most people didn't realize the foot markings after each stop indicated the pitch of the pipe and the length of the lowest pipe in that rank of 61 pipes. He set the stops for the

Swell manual. His choice was similar but not so bombastic. Just enough to contrast with the stops he'd chosen for the Great Manual.

He was ready to play. He began as fugues usually begin. He played the subject in the right hand and the soprano voice. Then he added the alto voice in contrast to the soprano. Third, was added the same subject melody in the tenor range. Finally the pedals.

By the time Otty got all four voices going in the fugue, he was aware that something was wrong. One voice didn't make much difference, but a full chord played together made a dreadful sound. The organ wheezed and grunted as if there was a squirrel or a bear running around between the pipes.

Otty stopped. Mercedes looked up. Even she, who was quite hard of hearing, noticed something was wrong.

Otty started again. This time he chose a hymn to play. "Maybe the old pipe organ isn't up for a fugue today," he thought. He played the first chords of "O God our Help in Ages Past" and the sound was even more dreadful. It was as if time had passed by the venerable organ with its glorious sound.

"What's wrong with that thing?" murmured Mercedes. Otty didn't hear her comment. He was more interested in finding out just what was going on. He slid off the organ bench and headed to the hidden door in the organ case below the façade pipes. The door led into the chamber where most of the pipes were. It was also a place where altar hangings and other worship ware, like candles, were stored.

He turned the key. Pulling on the latch, the big oak case door swung open. It was dark. He could barely see since the only light was that which filtered in between the façade pipes way above his head. He went in and closed the door behind him. He groped for the string that worked the one overhead incandescent light bulb. Finding it, he pulled and the light came on. Going from darkness to light, it took a moment for Otty's eyes to focus to the scene that lay before him.

Just about the entire set of pipes for the great manual were in disarray. They were crushed and bent every which way. Then he saw why. Lying in this tangle of organ pipes was Patchy Frost. She clutched one of the altar clothes in one hand. Obviously when she fell into the pipes she had reached out to grasp on to something. Instead of finding a sure hand hold, she stuck her hand into the edge of the swell shades that open and close on the front of the swell pipes. They closed on her hand. She lay unconscious and trapped by the pipes and swell shades of the magnificent instrument that could not speak in its present state. Patchy's body, now long dead and swollen from the heat in the airless organ chamber made it impossible to use the organ for any purpose until she was removed and the organ repaired.

Otty stood there in horror. He was kind of amused at the scene. Then a kind of satisfaction swept over him. He didn't much like Patchy. Not many people liked Patchy. But she didn't deserve this kind of end. More important, the organ didn't deserve this.

Patchy's eyes were fixated on something far off. Perhaps she died hearing the sounds of a celestial organ. Whatever had happened to her, this was or wasn't an accident. She could have committed suicide or, someone had it in for her and waited for an opportunity to do her in at a time when no one would be around except her. She certainly died in a place where it would be some time before she was found. By that time it was too late to save her. It was even too late for her body to lie in a casket, all prettied up with a big red rose in her hair. Patchy had gone beyond rigor mortis.

Otty felt guilty and sorry at the same time. He hadn't done anything to her. He was sorry. Probably he was the most sorry for the fact that his precious organ was now in shambles and the congregation that was to gather in an hour would have to live with a piano for accompaniment this Sunday.

Otty turned the light off and gently closed and locked the oak organ case door behind him. He headed to Rev. Brownell's study as Mercedes looked up from her bulletin folding. She was no wiser now than she was before.

"I have some news that's important," said Otty as he opened the door to Rev. Brownell's study. Brownell looked up and said, "What's that?"

"You'll have to come with me to see," said Otty. He motioned for Rev. Brownell to follow.

"What is it?" said Brownell.

"It's serious," replied Otty. "We'll have people coming in no time to worship and we have this problem with the organ. Should I say, we have the organ problem caused by another problem?"

Brownell rose and followed Otty down the stairs into the sanctuary by the back way. He led Brownell over to the oak door in the organ case and unlocking it they both stepped inside.

"Look!" said Otty.

"Look at what," said Brownell. "It's a pipe organ."

"Look over there," repeated Otty. "Over there in the pipes for the Great section of the organ."

Brownell looked and immediately felt faint. He saw it. He noticed it was Patchy only because she was wearing her familiar red rose in her hair. The rest of her had been lying there in the heat so long that she had been transformed from a human form into a bloated, purplish whale.

Stunned, Brownell stepped back and held on to Otty. The two stood there in the stench of the moment not knowing what to say or do.

"Well," joked Brownell, "at least she didn't go without that big red rose in her hair." When predicaments confronted him, Brownell often made a joke.

"This is no time for jokes," said Otty. "I tell you what we do right now. You and I are the only ones who know about this."

"And the person who did this," whispered Brownell.

"Right," continued Otty. "Since we are the only ones who know about this, I suggest we turn the light off, close the door, lock it and proceed with the morning worship service. I think the congregation is better off not knowing about this right now. We can deal with this after worship. I'll use the piano for singing. We'll tell the people that the organ has blown a bellows, or something like that."

Brownell thought a moment about Otty's proposal. "And your wife Vida can bring her cello and do some special music," said Brownell. "I'm game. Let's go for it. No need to disrupt 200 people who have come to worship. We can spare them the grief.They can learn about this in the papers. Agreed?"

"Agreed," said Otty. "I'll call Vida and ask her to bring her cello. She always has something ready to play."

The two walked away ready to resume their morning preparations as if nothing had happened. Before Brownell was too far away, Otty said, "Oh. And by the way, light some scented candles this morning. The perfume will cover up the scent of whatever needs covering up."

Brownell nodded approval and went back to his sermon. Otty opened up the grand piano and fiddled with the Bach Fugue, turning it into a piano piece. "That will be more interesting," he whispered to himself, "and the congregation will notice this version and complement me on my ability and creativity."

CHAPTER THIRTEEN

WORSHIP AS USUAL

"Where two or three are gathered together in my name, I am there among them." In addition to all sorts of motivations and chicanery. Matthew 18:20

Officer Gunnerson slipped into the back of the sanctuary to observe worship. He purposefully came late so as not to bump into Patchy Frost or anyone else he had conversed with since Ophelia's funeral the previous Tuesday. Otty Bourne had just finished the prelude. Vida, his wife was putting bow to cello in an offering of musical meditation. Rev. Brownell was already seated in his gothic minster chair, just awaiting the opportunity to speak the words of welcome.

He perused the sanctuary for anything that might stand out. The congregation appeared to be upper middle class, middle aged and senile. That was his first impression. He took the view of the congregation with a grain of salt and a little pepper mixed in.

"One never knows," thought Gunnerson, "what evil and chicanery lurks in the minds and hearts of women. No one is exempt for murder. The difference between someone who thinks about murder and someone who murders is in the doing." He closed his eyes and let the music coming from Vida and her cello descend over him.

"Gunnerson," he said to himself, "you are smarter than many think you are. Here you are in Loganwood because you knew enough to record a license plate number. And," he continued, "you're quite adept at analyzing persons and sensing guilt or not."

The music was coming to a close. He could see that Brownell was getting ready to take charge of the service.

Gunnerson's mind continued to wander and mingle with the words of greeting.

"This is the day the Lord has made. Let us rejoice and be glad." Announced Rev. Brownell. "We welcome you to First Church where the spirit is sometimes present, the congregation lurches and minds are weak." He didn't really say that. He did think it.

"That Patchy Frost," thought Gunnerson. "She was quite the character with her flamboyant red rose in her hair. You couldn't miss it. And that voice that went from sweet to drill sergeant. She's bossy. There's not much to like about her."

Otty, seated at the grand piano, began the introduction to the opening hymn. "All stand," ordered Brownell. Gunnerson stood. He wondered why they were using the piano for accompaniment. He had missed the announcement about the broken organ while he was deep in thought.

While the congregation half-heartedly sang the ancient words, *"O God, our help from ages past, Our hope for years to come,"* Gunnerson continued to evaluate the individuals gathered together and the gathering as a whole.

He was in the line of sight of Otty at the piano. "A funny fellow," thought Gunnerson. "He doesn't much like Brownell. He doesn't care for incompetent musicians. I suspect that he's just in this for the money or maybe to get his hands on that pipe organ."

The hymn was finished. The congregation was seated and looking attentive to what was happening at the pulpit. There was nothing unusual happening other than the usual. Prayers. Scripture readings. Announcements. Creed. Nothing meant much to Gunnerson. He was only there for observation. He suspected that nothing meant much too many who were gathered by the way he noticed they were responding or not responding. It was a pretty dull affair.

The offering plate came by. Gunnerson said "No Thank You!" as if he were being given something instead of being asked to give something. He passed it along. Others in the pew noticed. They always noticed when someone didn't make an offering. They were always more interested in what people could monetarily give rather than offering something like love. Many in the congregation judged each other and new people by what they wore, who they were, what they gave. They had learned that from many years of self-centered pastors. Rev. Brownell had encouraged it. He paid more attention to those with money than those in need.

"In the name of the Father, Son, and Holy Ghost," Gunnerson heard Rev. Brownell say. It was time for the sermon. The sermon title was "Love One Another." The platitudes out of Rev. Brownell's empty heart rolled over the congregation. Some heard. Most did not hear. Nothing was changed. Rev. Brownell's week away for respite, as he called it, hadn't made any difference in his preaching or motivation.

Gunnerson was reminded why he keeps a wide birth around churches and religion. He never did find love and forgiveness and God in church. He would much rather be sitting by a pond or a stream with a fishing pole in his hand. Nature was his sanctuary. Quiet his god. "Why do people listen to this?" thought Gunnerson. "What drivel? Does he really believe what he is saying?"

Gunnerson was thankful that the sermon only lasted fifteen minutes, for he was feeling uneasy sitting in that sanctuary with the scent of fragrant candles. There was something wrong but he couldn't put his finger on it.

With the strains of "Nearer My God to Thee," Gunnerson wondered if this church was actually sinking like the Titanic?

Only Otty Bourne and Rev. Brownell knew the truth behind the organ case during worship. Patchy Frost lay dead and rotting. The fragrant candles covered up any possibility of a foul odor that might weasel its way out between the organ façade pipes and settle over the innocent congregation.

"We got away with murder," said Otty to Brownell. "Well, not really murder. We got away without letting on that there had been either an accident or murder lurking behind those pipes. Once people are out of here, we'd better get Will Elwell in her to scoop up that Patchy Frost mess."

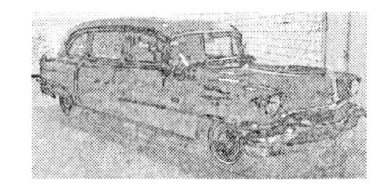

CHAPTER FOURTEEN

ALL'S WELL THAT'S ELWELL

Otty and Brownell couldn't wait for the congregation to disappear. Many stayed for fellowship time. Some noticed Patchy Frost was nowhere to be found. Some delighted that they were free from her orders and obnoxious flower and inappropriate intrusion into their conversations. A few missed her because they were amused by her. Otty and Brownell didn't miss her at all. They knew where she was.

"They're gone." Said Otty. "Now we've gotta deal with that dead body. You don't say anything, I won't say anything. Okay?"

"You got it," replied Brownell as he went to the phone in the kitchen to call Will Elwell at the Bartlett-Elwell Funeral home.

"Good Afternoon," answered Will in his most funereal voice. One could never be sure if it was friend, foe or customer who was calling.

"Hi Will," said Brownell. "This is Lee down at First Church."

"Oh Hi Lee," cheered up Will. He changed into his friendly, jovial voice. "What's up?"

"We've got a body down here at the church that needs to be removed. Can you come ASAP?"

"I'll be there in a dead man's second." Joked Will. Will could hear Otty in the background say, "Tell him it's a woman."

"It's a woman?" questioned Will. "Who is it? What happened?"

THERE'S A HEARSE IN MY PARKING SPACE

"Patchy Frost," replied Brownell. "Just get down her as quick as you can. Come in your service car, not the hearse. Park out back. The less visibility and publicity the better."

"I'm on my way." Replied Will.

Ten minutes seemed like an hour. It seemed especially long when you're holding your breath and trying to cover up a possible life-threatening scene that had already taken on life.

"We don't need that body lying there any longer than necessary," said Brownell. "Hurry up Will!" worried Brownell as he paced the floor.

"Now remember," said Otty. "We know nothing. We just found her dead. Who dunit or what happened, we know nothing."

"I know, I know," said Brownell.

Just then there came a loud rap on the backdoor that woke them out of their alibi and into the present moment. It was Will. He'd made it in record time.

"Where's the victim?" said Will as if it were all a joke. Somehow levity in a corpse situation like this helps. He knew lots of funeral parlor jokes and was ready to tell them at the drop of a hat, or a body, whichever came first.

"We don't need any jokes right about now," said Brownell getting more irritated and nervous by the moment. Just come follow us and clean up this mess.

Will followed them up the hallway from the kitchen into the sanctuary. He rolled along his stretcher and body bag to collect the corpse.

"In here?" Will asked somewhat confused. "In here in the sanctuary? Did you hear the one about the time the old lady died in the middle of worship. They carried out half the congregation before they found the dead woman." He laughed deep belly laughs. The joke didn't help the situation at hand.

"That's not funny right about now," said Brownell. Otty, on the other hand was having a hard time holding back a big, deep down belly laugh. Some of the weirdest things would strike him funny. He was more like Tim Conway on the Carol Burnett show in the middle of a hilarious skit than a serious mourner at a funeral.

"That's not funny," repeated Brownell, this time directed at Otty. "The body is in here." Brownell pointed to the Organ.

"In where?" asked Will.

"In there you dunce." Said Brownell. "She's in there and she's been there for some time. You're going to need more than that stretcher to get her out. I'd say a shovel and a hazmat bag would be more like it."

"That bad, huh?" said Will

"That bad. And if you can keep this whole thing quiet, I'll give you $1,000. Get her out of here and keep where she was found and what you saw out of the papers. We don't need any more bad publicity. The Ophelia Peden funeral was enough for one month."

Otty was stunned to hear the pastor offer a bribe. Then again, he wasn't that stunned. Brownell had been known to pay off people to get whatever he needed or wanted. For all he knew, Brownell could have been off on some toot the week before Ophelia's funeral and he'd paid someone to know and not know. Who knew? He didn't.

"Now Lee," began Will, "you know that I can't do that. I can't take a bribe to keep something quiet, especially if it's a situation that is less than on the up and up, if you know what I mean. Stop stalling and show me the body. Who is it anyway?"

"Patchy Frost." Said Otty.

Will was stunned by the announcement. Everyone knew Patchy Frost. She couldn't be missed. Her perfume and Red Flower in her hair always announced her coming and warned people to get out of her way. "Patchy Frost!" repeated Will. "Well I'll be. Let's see."

Otty unlocked the oak door in the pipe organ case and swung it open.

"I don't see anything," said Will. "It's dark in there. Where is she?"

The three of them stepped into the organ chamber. Otty turned on the overhead incandescent bulb. Will stepped back in horror. He might be a funeral director, a mortician, and he might have seen everything, but he hadn't seen anything quite like this.

Bloated and purple was an understatement. Sprawled out amongst all the bent pipes with her hand stuck in the swell box shades, which was rather curious.

"How did this happen? When did it happen? Who did this? Accident? Murder?" asked Will.

"I don't know the answer to any of those questions," said Brownell. I just know Otty found her earlier this morning and we thought it wise to keep it quiet and go ahead with worship until now. No need to upset the congregation that has gathered for worship. So there she is. Get her out of here and keep it quiet."

"I'll get her out of here but it's going to take some doing." Answered Will. "What a mess. We're going to have some time of it picking her out from among the pipes and you're going to have some time getting that historic organ repaired. Do you have insurance to cover something like this?"

"Don't be funny!" yelled Brownell. "What do you think about insurance? Who has insurance to cover a person being murdered and falling into pipes of a pipe organ and left to rot? Insurance, bah! Get her out of here and keep it quiet."

"Okay, Okay. Calm down." Said Will. "I'll get her out of here but I can't keep it quiet. At the very least there will have to be a death certificate and a funeral. What's the coroner going to put as the cause of death? "Went swan diving into a set of organ pipes and died?" I'm going to have to call the police. Sorry about that."

Brownell and Otty both knew that would have to happen. No amount of bribery could get around involving the authorities.

"I can call the police now or you can call the police." Said Will. "It's yours to decide. Me or you? I can't touch anything until the authorities have a look."

"I'll call" said Brownell in a resigned tone. He dialed his cell phone. The dispatcher answered.

"Loganwood Police Department," she answered. "How may I help you?"

"This is Rev. Brownell down at First Church," said Lee. "We have a situation here. Could the Chief come and ask her to please bring the coroner?"

"Is this a life or death situation?" asked the dispatcher. "Do you need an ambulance, police protection, what do you need?"

"It's beyond life of death," replied Brownell. "It's just death and we need the Chief and the coroner here as soon as possible."

"I'll send them. They'll be there within the hour," said the dispatcher. "It is Sunday so it'll take me a few to track them down. They'll be there."

Otty, Brownell and Elwell stepped out of the organ chamber into the sunlight streaming through the stained glass windows into the sanctuary. It was good to feel the warmth of the sun and to be away from the musty, hot, acrid air of the organ chamber. They also didn't much like Patchy belligerently staring at them through her swollen purple flesh. They waited in silence.

CHAPTER FIFTEEN

THE PICKLE PARK VISITOR

Gregg Morrison in Somewhere Maine was so enticed by Officer Gunnerson's visit that he decided it was worth the chance to violate his house arrest and probation. It was pretty easy to cut off the ankle monitor and leave it behind in his house.

"I won't get caught," thought Gregg. "By the time they realize I've been gone, I'll be back. No harm done." He jumped into his white pickup truck and headed out, driving I 95 South to Longwood outside of Boston.

It had been quite some time since he had been to the Boston area. Things had changed a lot. Living Downeast Maine and up some backwoods road doesn't afford one much time to get into the cultural life of a big city. Television reception isn't much good. It's pretty boring when the most interesting news is about a red tide coming in and the ban on clamming or that the lobster catch this year is too abundant. He didn't like Lobster anyway.

Gregg was a home grown boy with an imbecilic nature and little social skills. He wasn't quite sure what he was going to do once he got to Loganwood other than maybe by chance he would connect with the guy in the red pickup truck. Officer Gunnerson had given him just enough information to make him think that he might find the fellow. In finding the fellow, Gregg fantasized that it might lead to a pickle park type meeting or maybe an opportunity for blackmail.

Gregg was not above using any information he could gather about any person to use to his own advantage. He'd done it before and he'd do it again. Except for when he got entangled in the murder of Quentin Patel, he was quite successful at whatever scheme he cooked up. He couldn't seem to keep a job for very long, but what job he ever had, it was just long enough to screw up his employer and come out to his own benefit.

Gregg never learned his lesson. He tried the same thing over and over expecting different results. He'd succeed once or twice to make his pea-brained mind think that he could succeed every time. His escape from his house arrest and drive to Loganwood was just another incident of his making. He saw an opportunity and he decided to go for it.

In big cities like Loganwood there are places where people like Gregg and Rev. Brownell meet. Sometimes it's the Blue Hills outside Boston and not too far from Loganwood. Other times it's a local dive, motel or hang-out. Gregg didn't know about either place but he thought he'd find somewhere that might offer the opportunity to bump into this red pickup guy, Rev. Brownell.

For starters, he thought, he'd find the local Dunkin Donuts and hang out there.

CHAPTER SIXTEEN

THE LAW ORGAN-IZED

The wait for Chief Blanc seemed like hours. When one is nervous about a situation, ten minutes can turn into hours. It wasn't even ten minutes before the Chief arrived in an unmarked car. Because of the nature of the crime and its location, she didn't want to draw attention until she and others had an opportunity to gawk.

She parked around back and entered by the hidden side door that went directly into the hall to the sanctuary of First Church. Since Brownell had locked all the doors to protect the innocent and the dead, she had to knock with the butt of her billy club to get the attention of those hovering near the corpse. She could see the shadow of someone coming down the hall. It was Rev. Brownell.

"Come in," said Brownell in a guarded, yet official tone. "We've got quite a mess here. No one knows about this yet."

"Let's see what you have," said the Chief as she followed Brownell up the darkened hall leading to the altar area.

The door in the organ case, the way into the organ chamber, was open. Elwell and Otty stood at a distance from the opening trying as much as possible to avoid the stench that was beginning to filter between the organ pipes into the sanctuary.

"She stinks," said Elwell. "Be careful where you step. You might want to cover your nose with something."

"Been there, done this before," replied the chief as she stepped over the sill into the chamber dimly lit by one incandescent bulb high up in the ceiling.

"She's all yours," said Otty in a sarcastic tone. "She stinks, but that's nothing new. She always stank. If it wasn't from perfume it was from her attitude toward everything. She wasn't a very nice person."

Chief Blanc didn't say anything right away. She was making mental notes about the scene and what anyone was saying. So far Brownell hadn't said much. Otty had said too much.

"What do you mean?" the Chief finally asked Otty.

Otty was delighted to be asked his opinion. He didn't always have good judgment when it came to talking. He either preferred to influence others with his organ playing or talk incessantly when silence would have been more appropriate.

"Well," he began. "Patchy wasn't the nicest person to be around. She was always in everybody's face. She had an opinion about everyone and everything, whether you wanted to hear it or not." He paused. "And as far as her involvement in this congregation, she could be nice and helpful one minute and belligerent and bossy the next. People didn't always know how to react. When they saw her coming," he hesitated, "or smelled her coming, they would either become immobile or run the other way. Looks to me like someone got fed up with her."

The Chief made note of that conclusion. "What was she doing in the organ chamber anyway?" Asked the Chief. "Do you have any clue?" She listened for an answer as she bent over the corpse to stare into the blank eyes now almost covered by the drooping rose in Patchy's hair. "Pretty awful scene," said the chief.

She repeated, "What was she doing in the organ chamber?"

Brownell answered that one. "Some of the supplies for the altar are stored in here. Over there." He pointed. "She probably came in here to get some candles or altar clothes and tripped and fell into the organ pipes."

"I see." Said the Chief. "Is that something she did on a regular basis? Would there have been anyone with her?"

Brownell answered. "She had a key to the church and came in here whenever she felt the notion. She wasn't one to leave things to the last minute so she probably came in here anytime since the funeral that we had her on Tuesday. No one's been around much all week. The congregation and I were pretty warn out from dealing with that funeral. I didn't come in until Friday. I didn't notice anything then."

"I found her," said Otty. He couldn't wait to proudly announce that information.

"How did that happen?" asked the Chief as she looked from the corpse to Otty and back again to the corpse.

"I came in to practice the organ. When I turned it on everything seemed okay until I started to play. You should have heard the horrible noise it made. I went to investigate."

"And then you found her." Interrupted the Chief. "And what did you do?"

"I went to Rev. Brownell's office to tell him." Said Otty. "He came down and looked to."

"And neither of you," commented the Chief, "thought to call the police. And when you did decide to call, you called Will Elwell, the funeral director instead of the Police!"

Otty and Brownell stood there looking at the floor.

"We thought," said Otty, "that since it was so close to the time for worship that we should just close the door and lock it and go on with worship as if nothing had happened. Why put a congregation in an uproar when they had come to worship God?"

Chief Blanc thought that was a rather macabre move. "Of course the congregation didn't know they were worshiping with a dead body in their midst," she thought, "But then again, how many of those worshipers are actually aware of anything going on anyway. Most of them were half dead themselves or acted as if they were half dead." She looked at them with an amused look on her face, picturing the situation and remembering an old one liner joke she'd heard some years ago. She silently repeated it to herself. "Did you hear about the old lady who died in the middle of the worship service? They carried out half the congregation before they found her."

Chief Blanc chuckled.

"What are you laughing about?" Said Brownell.

"Oh nothing in particular," lied Chief Blanc.

Will Elwell stood off to the side waiting to scoop up Patchy and get out of there. He'd seen so many scenes like this in his career that neither the conversation nor Patchy's bloated corpse made any difference to him. In fact, he was thinking, "This will be an easy job. No makeup. No hair to fix. No clothing to put on the corpse. Just scoop her up, throw her parts into a body bag and off she goes. Of course the chief will want to have her carted off first for an autopsy."

That's exactly what Chief Blanc had in mind. "I'm going to record this as an accident for the time being," she said as she got out her report form. "However," she continued, "the body will have to go to the coroner's office for autopsy before a final determination can be made. We don't know if she fell by accident or if she was helped along. It's pretty obvious from the condition of the body that this happened some time ago. From the way she's sprawled out with her hand stuck in those venetian blinds,"

Otty interrupted to correct her. "Those are swell shades on the front of the swell pipe box. That's how you control the volume of the organ pipes." He said with authority.

"Whatever," said the Chief. She was getting perturbed by the attitude of the three standing around.

Brownell was nonchalant as if nothing had happened. He couldn't say it, but he was actually glad that Patchy would no longer be around to be a thorn in his side.

Otty with his "I'm the educated organist and know all about organs," attitude.

And Will Elwell leaning up against his gurney, anxiously tapping his toes and thinking, "Hurry the damn up. I have better things to do and money to be made where money is to be had." He tapped his toe on the hard wooden floor.

"Stop that!" yelled Chief Blanc. "I'll get the coroner here. Might as well call the press too so that they'll get the story straight before a rumor begins to circulate through your church members. They'll get it wrong for sure."

"You'll all have to hang around here until we get this body out and gone." She said as she called on her cell phone.

Otty sat down at the organ. "No point in trying to play. This thing is toast," he whispered to himself.

Brownell took a seat in the cathedral-like pulpit chair.

Elwell went out to the service car to wait and listen to the local broadcast of the Patriots football game. They were losing. It felt like everyone was losing right at the moment.

CHAPTER SEVENTEEN

SECRETLY CALLED

Dudley Nolan, to the less than better judgment of Rev. Brownell, had been nominated to be on the Staff-Parish Relations Committee. Brownell thought that he could trust Dudley. He also thought that with his business expertise, Dudley would be a good choice to help organize the staffing of the parish. Brownell had not thought very far into the future in that the Staff-Parish also is a place where kudos and gripes are aired, sometimes without the knowledge of the pastor. The members of the Staff-Parish were glad to have Dudley on board, so much so that they elected him chairperson.

When the headlines hit the paper, it was a total surprise to Dudley. He did some calling around of members of the congregation and he found out that no one else knew about Patchy's demise. The Loganwood Gazette was the first dissemination of that news. It couldn't be missed.

"Local Woman Found Dead in Church Organ Chamber"

Someone had leaked the news? There were only four people in on the discovery: Otty Bourne. Rev. Lee Brownell. Will Elwell, the Funeral Director. Chief Blanc. All had agreed not to say anything until a proper cause of death could be determined. When the Coroner had arrived, the Main Street of town was engaged in a sleepy Sunday afternoon. No one noticed him. The Patriots football game was on local TV and that drew the attention of many city residents. One of the team members was their star quarterback. He was from

Loganwood so people were naturally more interested in the game than what was happening down Main Street. The Coroner wouldn't have said anything. It would jeopardize his job.

Dudley Nolan, shocked at the news he read in the paper, decided that he'd had enough of Rev. Brownell's antics. Brownell had been away from the parish more often than not. When he was needed, he was nowhere to be found. Church members were being neglected at the expense of the life and existence of First Church. Office expenses were soaring through the roof and speaking of the roof, the church needed a new one. Dudley knew there were other misdemeanors of a church sort but the news headline occupied his time at the moment. It was time he took matters of the Staff-Parish Relations into his own hands and leadership instead of allowing Rev. Brownell to dictate the agenda.

Before doing anything rash, Nolan decided that he would make some calls to various members of the congregation. He also thought it wouldn't hurt to call some people in the community outside of the church. He wanted to test the waters in regard to the impression people were having about First Church and more specifically about Rev. Brownell.

Nolan chose carefully who he would call. The Mayor. The church treasurer. A supporter of Rev. Brownell. The waitress at the local Dunkin Donuts. Vida Hood, Otty's wife. Mercedes Hagenmacher. Marsha Hargrove, the church secretary. A few other people not so involved in First Church but regular worshipers.

It didn't take very many calls to discover that the church had a major problem on their hands. As usual, there are always people who have a favorable impression. Most of the time it is due to the experience they have had when a loved one has died and the pastor and the church has paid them particular attention. They have been helped to move through their grief.

On the other side of the story, there are always people who have an axe to grind. The usual subjects come up. The church talks too much about money. The pastor is never available. The organist plays too fast and too loud. The public address system is too loud or not loud enough. The sanctuary is too hot in summer and too cold in winter or vice versa. Many of the comments Dudley Nolan heard are trivial and worth ignoring. But others, well that was a different matter.

Nolan decided to call a meeting of the Staff-Parish, a secret meeting without the pastor. That was against the bylaw rules of the congregation and the denomination but he didn't care. People need space to tell the truth and their true feelings. They ought to do that in the presence of the person with whom they are having difficulty. However, that rarely happens. Church members are more prone to lie or give excuses than tell what they are really feeling and observing.

Nolan thought, "Maybe if we meet in secret without the pastor, or any other staff member for that matter, we'll get to the bottom of this.

Nolan set the meeting to happen on Tuesday. The body had been found on Sunday. The news hit the papers on Monday. Tuesday would give enough warning and enough time for the committee members to consider what they would say.

Nolan made the calls. Everyone agreed to attend. Each had read the Logan Gazette headlines. They knew why they were coming together. Not one asked why Rev. Brownell was not invited to be present. They kept the secret. And to be sure that the secret would not be discovered, Nolan was holding the meeting at his home. His wife Barbara was not a member of the committee, but she could sit on the side and provide refreshments.

For once every committee member was on time: Dudley Nolan, Calista McCann, and Arick Jansink. Kallie Jansink, wife of Arick, came along even though she wasn't a member. Esther Howlane and Thomas Dougal arrived together since Esther didn't drive. The committee was supposed to have nine members but Rev. Brownell neglected to find four more. In truth, no one wanted to be on any committee with Rev. Brownell. So an incomplete committee met.

CHAPTER EIGHTEEN

DONUTS AND ...

Gregg Morrison arrived late afternoon on Monday. He had googled the area for campgrounds and found there was a state campground two miles out of town. He easily found the place, paid his fee for camping the night and set up his site.

He drove into town in search of a coffee and to locate First Church. First Church wasn't hard to find. It was the big brick fortress of a building just ten feet off the sidewalk. It dominated Main Street. He was surprised to see that there was a hearse parked out front.

"Now what's going on," he thought as he was reminded of the murders that had happened back home in Maine. "I'll come back and pay that church a visit sometime this week before I head home."

Gregg drove the length of Main Street taking note of the businesses along either side. There were lots of folks out walking in the beautiful early evening sunlight. Most of the spaces were occupied with parked cars. "Must be an upscale city," commented Gregg to himself. "Look at the Audis, BMWs, Buicks, and Caddies. Well it is close to Boston. Must be most people work in the city."

On his way down Main Street in search of a coffee shop, Greg noticed a Dunkin Donuts in the middle of the block not too far from the church. Even at this late hour of the day there were lots of cars parked there. DD had no drive up window so he pulled into the lot and parked the truck right out front. As he walked to the door he noticed a red pickup truck parked three spaces from his truck. The visit from Officer Gunnerson to his house a few days before came to mind. That was the reason he had driven to Loganwood in the first place. It was a coincidence, or was it, that there would be a red pickup truck parked at the very first place where he parked. Gregg wondered if it was the same truck that he had noticed at the pickle park back home. He knew what the man was doing at the pickle park. Until Officer Gunnerson came to visit, he had very little idea who the man was.

Gregg pulled the door open and entered. He was greeted by the fresh aroma of dark roast coffee, the new DD flavor. He was pleased to see that this DD was offering all things pumpkin flavor since it was autumn and getting close to Thanksgiving.

"May I help you," said the clerk.

"I'd like a medium dark roast with cream and two of those pumpkin donuts, please." Replied Gregg.

Gregg surveyed the room. There were just a few tables. An elderly lady sat at one. "Must be one of those bag ladies," Gregg thought to himself. "Look at all that stuff she's got piled up around her in garbage bags."

He avoided that table and chose one on the other side of the room and just a table away from two men sitting, drinking their coffee and having conversation. He was glad to have a moment to relax, take his time and drink his coffee before going back to his campsite.

"I can't say I'm going to much miss her," Gregg heard one of the men say. "She was an awful nuisance and that perfume always gave me a headache."

"I can understand that," said the other man," but we should always give persons the benefit of the doubt. They are children of God, you know."

"Well," said the other man, "I understand that but sometimes God just puts the most annoying people in front of us, or in church. I'm so tired of dealing with crazy people. I'm fed up with trying to keep a church alive. It's time I had a life of my own. "

"Now, Lee," said the other man. "You need to develop some patience. Maybe you need to take a leave of absence or an extended vacation. How about a sabbatical. You do have some wonderful things to offer us at church. And..."

"And what?" interrupted the other man.

Gregg thought to himself, "This is getting very interesting. Who are these men? They obviously have some kind of relationship. They have something to do with church." Gregg leaned over his coffee and took a bite out of his pumpkin donut all the time listening more carefully to the conversation. He cupped his hand behind one ear, the better to hear.

"Well Tom," said the man named Lee to the other, "I'm fed up with doing 24/7 duty and babysitting people who can't make a decision for themselves. The only good thing about that woman is that she used to tell everyone else what to do so that I didn't have to do it. The bad thing about her is that she used to tell me what to do, especially when it was none of her business. She was a busy body."

"Now Lee," replied the man named Tom, "you know as well as I, you've preached on it, that everyone is a child of God. You can't dismiss someone so easily, even if they are annoying and a thorn in your side."

"I know that," replied the man named Lee, "but this time she's not just a thorn in my side. She's a big spike right in my gut. She's an arrow in my heart. What am I going to do now that she's been found dead? And not only dead, dead in the organ. She ruined the organ and that's going to cost us a ton of money."

"Lee," said Tom. "Stop that. You're just going to have to buck up and deal with all the guilt, all the rumors, all the crazy behavior, all the innuendo that is going to come your way. And if it gets too bad, you can always take a week off and go up country or to the beach, somewhere where you can think."

Gregg finished his coffee and donuts just about the time the two men appeared to be finishing up their conversation. It sounded like they hadn't resolved anything. "Sometimes," thought Gregg, "all a fellow needs is someone to unload on, talk to, and get some sympathy. Advice is in order as well."

"Let's go," said the man named Lee. "I'll drop you off at your house."

Gregg watched the two men leave. To his surprise, and amusement, they headed to the red pickup truck. Lee got in. They drove off.

CHAPTER NINETEEN

A LITURGY FROM HELL

Two days had passed since Patchy was found. Will Elwell had come and scooped her up. Chief Blanc had made her preliminary notes, photographing and describing the scene.

Otty had gone home to his sterile and sexless life with his wife. He got no sympathy from her. Up until his arrival back home, she didn't even have a clue what was going on. She just thought the organ had lost its wind.

Brownell was shaken because he was now into a marathon of funeral, worship, funeral, investigation, and goodness knows what else was going to happen in the space of a week or two. It was one of those minister schedules that he so hated about his job. When things were good, they were very good. When things started to go downhill, they went as fast as an Olympic skier on Mount Washington. "Too often skiers, and hikers for that matter," he thought, "end up lost or dead on Mount Washington." He also knew that things like this happened in threes. "Who is going to be the third? Or what is going to be the third bad thing to happen?"

Brownell felt sorry for himself. His life was always being interrupted by something he'd rather not do or deal with. When he had arrived home on Sunday afternoon his wife was there. She barely looked up from the book she was reading. It was one of those "I couldn't care less that you are home, moments." He tried to make conversation with her. She wasn't interested, until he mentioned that Patchy was found dead. Even that news barely got a rise out of her. "No sex or sympathy from her," he thought as he climbed the stairs to take a Sunday afternoon nap. That was Sunday at the parsonage.

Time had passed slowly between his fitful Sunday afternoon nap and Tuesday morning at the office. Nothing had changed at home. Much had changed with the church and Patchy.

The rumor mill was in good working order. Someone had leaked information to the press about Patchy's demise. No details were told but a small article at the bottom of the front page of the Loganwood Gazette enticed the community. It also scared some people that there might be a murderer on the loose.

"WOMAN FOUND DEAD" was the headline. In a short paragraph it was reported that she had been found dead at First Church on Sunday afternoon and that there was an investigation in progress. The article didn't name the deceased for the usual reason that next of kin hadn't been notified. There were no next of kin. Or at least, no next of kin was willing to admit that they were kin of Patchy Frost, the woman with smelly perfume, a domineering personality and a red rose! The article didn't need to name Patchy as the victim. Whoever leaked the information, had already spread her name throughout the congregation. Neither Rev. Brownell nor Chief Blanc were happy about this rumor.

Will Elwell contacted Rev. Brownell that something needed to be done with Patchy's remains, what was left of her after the autopsy that was done on Sunday evening. "We've got to get her wrapped up and in the ground," said Elwell when he telephoned Brownell on Monday evening.

Brownell agreed. Since there was no next of kin, and friends lived far away, and Ophelia, her closest friend was dead, the planning for the funeral was left to Brownell and Otty. "Words and Music," that'll be enough thought Brownell.

The planning meeting was Tuesday morning with the funeral to be on Thursday. Otty arrived a few minutes late.

Marsha Hargrave, the secretary was already there, as was Brownell. Lee had also asked Mercedes Haggenmacher to come and represent the congregation and Barbara Nolan to represent the lady's society.

They sat in the outer office with one of the church's Tiffany stained glass windows casting a soft light on the group. Jesus, holding a lamb, stared down at them. It was one of those portrayals of Jesus in glass that had eyes that seemed to be looking directly at you, no matter where you sat. Brownell sat with his back to the window. He didn't much like being stared at, especially from Jesus.

Barbara Nolan was in one of her "I'll get this organized mood," and "don't tread on me." She sat listening and staring at the face of Jesus. She was obviously in one of those guilt moments. Not many people connected her unsympathetic behavior with the fact that she felt guilt over the death of her daughter some years before in a horrific car crash. When she got into that depression, it oozed out over everyone and everything. It was unfortunate that she was having one of those moments right when sympathy was more in order.

Mercy listened carefully. Ever since her cataract operation she claimed she could hear well. Brownell laughed when she'd said that in worship one Sunday. He knew she was a little simple but a gentle and merciful soul. He asked her to be at the planning because she would add some mercy and kindness to the service.

Brownell opened the meeting. "I'll do the standard funeral service," he said. "Prayers, scripture, eulogy." "We won't have Patchy to interfere in the planning and execution of this one" he thought to himself.

Otty, ever creative, said, "I'll play Bach's Toccata and Fugue in D. Minor for the prelude."

"You WON'T play that!" said Barbara and Brownell in unison. "What do you think this is, Halloween?" said Barbara.

Marsha Hargrave made a note. Of course she wouldn't include that comment in the funeral bulletin but she wanted to remember it so she could tell her husband. They'd both have a good laugh at Patchy's expense.

"Well then," said Otty. "What do you want me to play for gathering music?

"How about that same damn thing you played at Ophelia's." He didn't actually say "damn." But he thought it. "You know," he continued. "That dirge of a thing. That lost something or other that should have been lost decades ago."

"The Lost Chord," said Otty. "Okay, I'll play that. And for Detroit music," the others laughed. He was always calling coming in and going out music "Introit's and "Detroits." He continued, "For Detroit music I'll play "Arrival of the Queen of Sheba."

"You won't either,"said Barbara. Brownell was amused but said, "Come on, Otty, stop this and let's get this meeting over with."

"How about "Dance Macabre," or "To a Wild Rose," or "The Last Rose of Summer?" Brownell knew what he was getting at. Otty was remembering what Patchy looked like lying there in between the organ pipes, all bloated, purple with a rose in her hair.

The others didn't have a clue. Marsha let out a guffaw and immediately went back to taking notes.

"Cut it out!" said Brownell and Barbara in unison. "Get serious," continued Brownell. "You've got to play something appropriate or we'll have the denominational authorities on our backs and charging us with something. You know how stupid they can be. Some fool will file a complaint, they'll have a trial of both you and me, and we'll be out, defrocked, de-organized. Get serious."

Otty understood what Brownell was getting at. Neither he nor Brownell could let on they knew more than anyone else about Patchy's demise. In addition there had been way too much publicity nationally and internationally about renegade people in the church filing charges against ministers for violation of one church law or another. There had even been a case where a trial was held that had cost the denomination over 100,000 dollars and ended in lots of people leaving. With the current state of society and the denomination it looked like the church was either going to capitulate to the Holy Spirit moving it forward or give in to the screamers insisting on black and white laws. It looked like a split was in the future of the denomination and no one could predict what a local church would do. Brownell was very aware of that. He needed to keep this Patchy Frost thing under control. He wanted his pension more than integrity, honesty and truth.

"Then how about I do a medley of hymns as people Detroit it out?" Said Otty. "And as they roll the casket down the aisle I'll strike up with "When the roll is called DOWN yonder, she's there." He doubled over with laughter.

"Cut it!" said Brownell. "A medley of hymns will be fine. No funny business. And maybe you can find some stops on the organ that still work. If not, the Piano."

With the order of the service settled, Barbara Nolan said she'd take care of the refreshments. She would just tell the ladies what to do. Now that Patchy was out of the picture, Brownell was sure that Barbara would take over being the thorn in his side. He did, however, know that she would follow through.

Mercedes didn't offer anything specific. She could be counted on to fold the bulletins, welcome people and be a calm presence in the midst of a raging storm.

"Good then, we're done. See you at the show." Said Brownell. They just barely heard that comment made under his breath as they left the meeting. Brownell couldn't wait to get out of the church, out of his pastoring clothes, and head for Dunkin Donuts for his mid-morning break.

CHAPTER TWENTY

A POLICE REPORT

Brownell's cell phone rang. He was sitting at Dunkin Donuts enjoying a cup of coffee and a cinnamon-raisin bagel. "Damn," he thought, "I can't even have a moment of peace. It never fails. The phone rings at the worst times."

"Hello," he answered in a low voice as there were other people at other tables.

"Rev. Brownell," said the voice on the other end. "This is Chief Blanc. I have some bad news. Can you talk?"

"Not very well," replied Brownell. "I'm at Dunkin Donuts. You can talk. I'll listen."

"I have some bad news. Just listen and we'll plan to meet soon. Probably Wednesday." Said the Chief.

"We're doing the funeral Thursday morning," he said in his best "I-don't-want-others-to-hear-this" voice. "Can you tell me the news over the phone? And then meet?

"Let's just say it looks like Ms. Frost died under less than normal circumstances. I'll fill you in. Is 1 pm good?"

"Yes," said Brownell.

"Good. Come down to the station where we can talk in private." Replied the Chief.

"I'll see you then," replied Brownell as he heard her hang up the phone on the other end.

Brownell's blood pressure began to rise. It always rose in situations like this. When he visited the doctor for his yearly physical, he started working on his blood pressure the night before. The doctor didn't believe him until one year he took his blood pressure every day for two weeks before the visit. It was always very low or normal. He also noticed that his blood pressure was very low after the stress of worship on Sunday morning was over. "Maybe I should start checking my blood pressure this week," he thought. "With all the upset of the past three weeks, and now this, I bet my blood pressure is through the roof."

During the phone call, Gregg Morrison had come in for his morning coffee and to scope out the scene. He watched Rev. Brownell drive off in his red pickup truck. "He must have a daily routine of coffee and a donut each day." He thought. "I'll be here a little earlier tomorrow and see if I can connect with him."

CHAPTER TWENTY ONE

A SECRET MEETING

They all arrived on time for the Staff-Parish meeting. Barbara Nolan had set out a lovely table of cookies and tea. She wasn't part of the committee but it was not above her to sit on the fringe and to offer a comment now and then. Too often her comments related to her guilt over her daughter's death. Occasionally, since she was an English teacher, she offered some bit of wisdom.

Dudley perched his girth on the sturdiest chair in the living room. He had become morbidly obese from years of sitting behind a disk as president of the Loganwood Trust. It didn't' help either that he and Barbara had long since given up sex. He was too heavy to be on top her and she was too controlling and lazy to do otherwise. To say that Dudley was fat was an understatement. On the upside, he was a good, intelligent and capable man. Highly respected in the community, he was always at the top of the candidate list when someone needed a chairperson, worker or committee member. That was one of the reasons Rev. Brownell had fingered him for the Staff-Parish.

Dudley was fair to the letter. But if something was not on the up-and-up, as was the case this evening, he could be brutally honest and ruthless in his dealing with issues.

Dudley checked his attendance sheet: Mercedes Haggenmacher (Mercy), Calista McCann, Thomas Dougal, Esther Howlane, Kallie and Arick Jansink. "Good," said Dudley, "We're all here. Let us pray."

That was something unusual for the group. Rev. Brownell rarely, if ever, began meetings with prayer. But the group bowed their heads and obliged. Several stared at the floor for fear that Dudley was going to ask them to pray. He didn't so he prayed.

"Eternal God, Father of us all," he began.

"I wish," thought Kallie, "that they'd stop this father, male crap. I had enough of that when I was a Catholic."

Dudley continued. *"We are gathered here in this secret room just as you gathered your disciples together in a secret upper room the night before you were betrayed. Not one of us is innocent. We all live lives that move between grace and sin. Forgive us for this gathering but grace us with your presence. Give us wisdom and kindness. Give us insight and truth. Help us, help your church, to be all that you would have us to be. In the name of Jesus. Amen."*

Quiet descended upon the little group. Silence. Not one there had ever heard Dudley pray. Not one knew that he even had those kinds of words within his heart. They pondered what he had prayed. A seriousness came over each. Each knew that they were meeting in violation of their membership oath, to uphold and encourage each other. Each knew that to meet in secret without the knowledge of the person they would be discussing was less than grace-filled and merciful. Each knew. But they met anyway.

Dudley began. "We are gathered here as God's people to do God's work. We must be all about integrity, even though we are meeting in silence. Whatever conversation we have here tonight must stay here until such time as it is needed. What happens in my house tonight stays in this house. Does everyone understand?"

Dudley asked each individually if they agreed. When all had answered in the affirmative he explained the reason for the meeting.

"Over the past months I have received a number of comments and complaints from members and people in the community about our church and our pastor. Some of the comments are nothing but rumor. Some of the comments I hope are nothing but rumor. Some of the comments are issues we need to deal with and either counsel our pastor or advise him to seek whatever is needed for him and us."

Dudley pulled a stack of papers upon which he had typed three areas of concern he felt needed to be discussed. He handed a copy to each member and then listed the areas on a flip chart.

"The issues we need to discuss this evening in regard to our pastor and our church involve three major concerns. They are," as he began to write on the flip chart. "Financial Irresponsibility. Mismanagement or abuse of members. "Accountability – accountable to no one." You have them listed on the paper I handed out. We'll discuss each one at a time. You can make notes, but I want the papers back so that our conversation stays in this room."

Dudley perused the circle. Connecting eye to eye with each there, he said, "Understood?" Each replied in the affirmative. "Good, then. Let us begin with Financial Irresponsibility. What comments have you heard or what are your impressions about the finances of our church?"

Arick Jansink didn't hesitate to get in on this topic. His secular job involved financial records. "I think," He said, "that we have major financial problems. We never know where we stand financially. The weekly bulletin always shows a deficit. We take in less money than we spend. And when we do have enough money we are always giving it away to missions and yearly assessment to the denomination instead of taking care of our bills locally."

"I understand that," said Calista, "but it is important that we help those less fortunate than ourselves. If we don't help others, we'll not be able to take care of ourselves."

"I don't buy that at all," said Arick. "We need to be taking care of ourselves. If there's anything left over, then we can help others."

Tom Dougal said, "I'm concerned at how the pastor just seems to go to church members and hit them up for money. I found it especially surprising when he announced that we had taken out a $55,000 loan to repair the steeple and that it was interest free for six months. Where'd he get that money? Why is it all hush-hush and anonymous? I suspect that he got a loan from a church member. If that is the case, it will all backfire. We'll lose that member. We won't be able to pay it back. I think that is not only financial irresponsibility, it's mismanagement and abuse of a member."

"What do the rest of you think?" asked Dudley.

"I agree," said Esther Howlane. "My husband who wouldn't darken the door of this or any church has said the same thing. Too many churches, including ours, is controlled by a pastor who does everything and controls everything. I was surprised and delighted when he asked me to be the Congregational Leader. It made me feel important and useful. He doesn't often allow that."

"I don't think it is a good idea for him to just do what he wants," said Kallie Jansink. "We've been wanting to have a map of the world in the foyer for a long time. I was on the trustees and we discussed where to put it. When I wasn't at a meeting one night, somehow he got the trustees to agree to put it right out there in the hall where you can't miss it. I didn't want it there and would have said so. A week later when I asked him about it and said that I thought he had put it there, he got up from his desk, walked to me and said, "You Know what this is, This is Bullshit!" He then followed me to the front door, opened it and said, "Don't let it hit you on the way out!"

The rest didn't dare respond to Kallie probably because most of them knew that when she confronted the minister she probably <u>was</u> full of bullshit. It didn't matter that they agreed with her story. What they didn't agree with was the bullshit that Kallie often dished out. More than once she was heard yelling at some church member because something was done she didn't like. People were afraid of her. The truth be known, she was delighted that Dudley had called this secret meeting. Finally she would have a platform and opportunity to push her agenda which has always been "to bring down the minister, get him defrocked or get him moved."

"What do the rest of you think?" asked Dudley.

"I think," spoke up Mercy, "that we have a very good minister who isn't perfect. Sometimes we can't find him but he does need to have time for renewal. Sometimes he does things that seem odd or not Christian, but we do need to trust him for his leadership. He has done some great things."

"Mercy!" said Esther, "Mercy, mercy, mercy. You are always looking on the bright side of life. How Pollyanna. It's good to have that in small doses, but we're in a situation where we have to look at the reality of what's happening. Our finances are a mess. We owe too much money. The denomination thinks we are on our way out. People have left for our neighbor church across the street. One of our old members comes to church on Sunday morning, parks in our parking lot which is labelled for PAYING MEMBERS, walks in the back door of our church, through the sanctuary, picks up a bulletin, goes out the front door and worships across the street. And now on top of it all, we're in the news twice in the last week. Ophelia is burned up in a fire in Maine. And now Patchy. Sure Patchy was a nuisance but she got things done. Maybe she was one of the controls we had left on our minister. She was always on him to make sure he did what was supposed to be done ... in her mind and heart."

The group sat in silence. Dudley let the pause descend over the group. Finally he spoke. "And let me add," he said, "Not one of us is free from the responsibility for what has been happening in our church. It takes more than one person for things to happen. Listen, each of us in our own way has participated in what has brought us to this point in our church."

"I don't think so," countered Kallie.

"I do," said Calista. "Dudley is right. Each of us has participated either by doing something or doing nothing. Instead of assisting our minister and helping in areas where he is incapable of, we have let him fall. In letting him fall and fail, we fail too."

"Well, isn't that just sweet Pollyanna thinking," Snarled Kallie."

"Oh please don't attack each other," pleaded Mercy. "Let's have some love and kindness in solving our problems."

"That's right," said Dudley. "We can view our finances and our member relations as an opportunity for us and for our pastor, or we can just become a shark tank that devours each other. Let's try to be constructive instead of destructive."

"Good Luck," said Kallie.

"I'm game," said Arick. The group, however, didn't quite believe that. Whereas his wife, Kallie was blatantly aggressive, Arick was passive aggressive. He would often say one thing and mean and do just the opposite. He was not to be trusted. Most people thought, and rightly so, that probably the only way he and Kallie got along was the clash of their passive and aggressive personalities. Some thought, "It must be interesting for them in the bedroom."

"So," said Dudley, "I am hearing that we have some specifics that we can discuss with the pastor. I think that we can talk with him about how he manages the members of the congregation. We can discuss in depth the financial workings of our church and that also involves accountability. We are the staff-parish relations committee responsible for accountability. It is time, I think, that we stand up for God and ourselves and our church and we work with the pastor to put in place some systems to help him be accountable. In the same way, we need to be accountable to each other and the congregation. They are depending upon us for good pastoral leadership. In fact they are depending upon us for good staff. Do you all agree?"

Tom Dougal said, "I think you are correct. We have let these situations go for too long. We haven't had the grace or courage to talk with our pastor. We've allowed him to set the agenda instead of us working together. The sooner we meet with him the better. And the quieter we keep the fact that we've had this meeting the better."

"I'm in total agreement of that," said Calista. "If word gets out to him that we've had this meeting he will be furious and we will suffer his wrath and we'll get nowhere."

"Agreed?" said Dudley. "Then as far as we are all concerned, this meeting hasn't happened. Once Patchy's funeral is over and the congregation has a little time to settle down, we'll have a meeting with the pastor. How about next Sunday Evening?"

There was consensus that this was a good plan. Dudley indicated that he would speak with Rev. Brownell, indicating there would be a meeting Sunday as an opportunity for discussion and helpfulness.

"Let us Pray," said Dudley. *"Dear God. Thank you for your presence. Draw us together in your love. Empower us to witness to your grace. Forgive us our sins and make us your kind and loving servants to your glory. Amen.*

Dudley had been eyeing the refreshments that Barbara had laid out, so he was relieved when she shouted.

"BEFORE YOU ALL LEAVE, eat some of this stuff or take some home. DUD is fat enough already."

They laughed, thankful for the refreshments and Barbara's injected levity.

CHAPTER TWENTY TWO

A CHANCE MEETING

Gregg Morrison was already at Dunkin Donuts when Rev. Brownell arrived around 10 am on Wednesday. He wasn't sure if Brownell came every morning but he didn't want to miss his chance to connect with him. From what he observed down home in Maine, he thought there might be a good chance that he could become Brownell's new reason for going to Maine. He had information about Brownell that he was sure the people in Loganwood and at First Church would love to get their little mitts on. He could just imagine what the newspaper headlines would be.

"Local Minister Caught Behind the Bushes"

"Prominent Clergy Found Arrested With His Pants Down"

Gregg chuckled to himself as he sat drinking his coffee and contemplating biting into his pumpkin donut. There was no rush. He could milk his coffee for as long as need be, hoping that his prey would appear.

He didn't have to wait long. Brownell arrived about 10:15. He was such a frequent customer that the lady behind the cash register had his order prepared and waiting as soon as she saw him drive up in his red pickup truck.

"Good Morning, Reverend," she said. "I hope you're up for a great new day."

"We'll see about that," growled Brownell. "Another funeral to deal with. This is getting tedious."

"I'm sorry to hear that," she replied. "Anyone I know?"

"If you knew her, you wish you didn't know her." He retorted. "Patchy Frost. The bossiest person on the planet. I never thought I'd be doing her funeral. Now I have to think of something nice to say about her."

"You'll do fine," said the cashier. "You always do." She always had a word of encouragement for customers. Besides, she didn't want to have this conversation turn into a pity party and an answer on an essay test.

Gregg watched as Brownell took his coffee and cinnamon raisin bagel to the table next to the window and facing Gregg. They just barely acknowledged each other's presence.

The moment seemed ripe for the picking. Gregg said, "It sounds like you are having the kind of day I'm having. Perhaps two can make something whole out of the day. May I join you?"

At first Brownell was surprised but thinking there was no harm in the good looking man joining him at his table, he agreed. Gregg moved over.

"My name is Gregg Morrison," he said. "I'm visiting in town for a few days. I heard this was a nice place to visit. More to do here than downeast."

"Downeast?" said Brownell. "Maine?"

"Yes," replied Gregg. "I live a long way out in the sticks. Ayah, it's quite a place. Not much to do there than to hang out in the woods, watch the trees grow and notice the comings and goings of people." He paused. "You ever been to Maine?"

"Yes." Replied Brownell with a kind of hesitation that indicated the conversation seemed a little suspicious. "Matter of fact I just got back from there. I like to take my pickup truck and go off to see what kind of change of scenery I can find. How about you?"

"I like to hang out in the woods too." Said Gregg. "I have a pickup truck. That white one out there. What kind of truck do you have?"

"That red pickup." Replied Brownell. Matter of fact, I'm parked right next to yours. I thought I noticed Maine number plates when I drove up."

"You ever been to Somewhere Maine?" asked Gregg.

Brownell shivered. He'd just gotten back from there. The conversation was taking an odd turn. He was feeling nervous about continuing the conversation there in public. Usually a church member or someone who knew him would come in for their morning coffee. He didn't want to cause suspicion by people seeing him sitting with a stranger. The stranger named Gregg seemed harmless and beside he was handsome and it had been sometime.

"Tell you what," said Brownell. "You're new in town. I've got the morning off. How about we go for a ride in my pickup and I'll show you the area and we can talk without the listening ears of anyone in here?"

"Great idea," said Gregg as he bagged up his uneaten donut and put the lid on his coffee. Brownell did the same.

"See you later, maybe," waved Brownell to the Cashier. She was busy with other customers so she barely acknowledged that she had heard.

Gregg jumped in, found the cup holder and planted his coffee on the dash of the red pickup. Brownell started the engine, backed out and they were off.

"I know some really pretty spots around here where we can park, have our coffee and not be disturbed." Said Brownell. He was curious about Gregg. He had some less than honorable thoughts about what they might do once he'd found the pull off he was thinking about. He headed down Main Street, turned up Elm that lead out of town. About a mile out of town he turned up a road less travelled. It wound its way into the forested countryside and along a river. Going up a slight hill and around a curve, Gregg could see that they were coming to a spot where the river veered off to the right. There was a pull off hidden from the road. A short path led down into the woods. Brownell occasionally visited the spot to think and.

"Beautiful spot," said Gregg. "Do you come out here often?

"Only when nature calls," said Brownell. "You know what I mean?"

"I guess." Replied Gregg. "I have a special place back home where I go to find myself. Occasionally someone finds me."

"Finds you?" prompted Brownell.

"Yes. I'm not the only one who likes that pull off just south of Somewhere. Some days there's quite a lot of in and out traffic. I like it. You never know who you are going to find or what you are going to see happening."

They had gotten out of the red pickup and Brownell indicated that there was a nice spot at the edge of the ravine overlooking the Stone River. There was a place to sit. The sun was warm and they could chat more there.

Brownell led. Gregg followed. "It's a beautiful river down there, isn't it?"

"Sure is." Replied Gregg. Considering the way the conversation was going he thought it was about time that he indicated that he knew more than Brownell thought he knew.

"You ever been to Maine?" said Gregg. "You ever been to Somewhere Maine?"

Brownell hesitated. The question a second time surprised him. Thinking it was no harm in telling the truth, he replied, "Yes. Matter of fact, I was there just recently."

"We don't have much excitement there," said Gregg. "Once in a while there is some goings on that gets in the news and makes the place interesting. Did you hear about the big fire we had a while back? Burned our old historic inn right to the ground! And took a woman with it. Burned up like toast in a short circuited toaster."

"Really?" said Brownell. "Come to think of it, it is a small world. I officiated at the funeral of that woman who got burned up. Nothing but sad, sad, sad."

"Small world!" repeated Gregg as he thought that he now had Brownell in his pocket, so to speak. "I think I saw your red pickup more than once that week of the fire. Didn't I see you at the pickle park pull off? I was crouched down in a thicket up near an open field."

A shiver went up and down Brownell's spine. "What was this guy getting at," he thought. "How much does he know?"

They stood there in silence at the edge of the ravine. The sun sparkled through the trees. "It is a lovely morning for a walk in the woods. I love the poetry of Robert Frost. Do you know his poem, "The Road Less Travelled?" he asked Gregg.

"I do." Replied Gregg as he started to recite it.

"Two roads diverged in a yellow wood,
And sorry I could not travel both"

Brownell joined in as they spoke it in unison.

And be one traveller, long I stood
And looked down one as far as I could
To where it bent in the undergrowth;

Then took the other, as just as fair,
And having perhaps the better claim,
Because it was grassy and wanted wear;
Thought as for not the passing there
Had worn them really about the same.

They paused in the recitation as the sun had swung higher in the sky and bathed warmth on their shoulders. It was a John Denver, "Sunshine on your Shoulders" moment. Gregg continued

*And both that morning equally lay
In leaves no step had trodden black.
Oh, I kept the first for another day!
Yet knowing how way leads on to way,
I doubted if I should ever come back.*

Brownell joined in.

*I shall be telling this with a sigh
Somewhere ages and ages hence:
Two roads diverged in a wood, and I ---
I took the one less travelled by,
And that has made all the difference.*

"And that has made all the difference," repeated Brownell in a melancholy tone. "All the difference."

He looked at his watch. "I must get back to town for a meeting. I'm glad we met. Thank you."

The sunlight and the ravine was left to its own purpose for the day. Two roads diverged that made all the difference for that day.

CHAPTER TWENTY THREE

AT THE POLICE STATION

Officer Gunnerson from Somewhere Maine brushed against Rev. Brownell as he was leaving. Chief Blanc had called him in to solicit his assistance. She thought it might be good to have someone unknown to the community involved in what now appeared to be more than just an accident in the organ chamber at First Church.

"Thanks for coming." Commented Chief Blanc as he passed Brownell on the way in. "Come in, Rev. Brownell," she said as she transitioned from one interview to another.

The Chief's office was pleasant enough but still it was a police office. There was no reason for Brownell to suspect anything. He was there to find out what the coroner had to report.

"The report came back from the coroner on Patchy Frost." Said Chief Blanc. "I thought it best that I tell you first before rumors get circulating around this city. You know how people are. Already people are talking and they know nothing."

"Typical people." Commented Brownell. "Church is the same. One person says something. Another person overhears something. Pretty soon a mountain is made out of a mole hill and people and churches are destroyed."

"Exactly," said the Chief.

"So what's the report say," asked Brownell.

"Murder." Replied the Chief as she made a note of how Brownell reacted to the news.

"Murder! Oh," he shouted and then mumbled something under his breath. "Now the rumors will be flying" he commented. "Why did they conclude murder?"

"Someone hit her over the head with a very heavy object." Said the Chief. "She wasn't just in that organ chamber to get altar hangings. She was hit over the head and fell into the organ. The fall didn't kill her. Someone else did. She just happened to be barely alive when she fell into the organ pipes and died."

"I can't imagine what it's going to cost to get that organ rebuilt." Said Brownell. "There's always something and now this. It's just like Patchy to have one last swan song to control the church and everything around her. Damn." He often thought more of money than persons.

"So, now this death has turned to a murder investigation." Continued the Chief. "They figured this happened on Thursday and by the time Otty Bourne found her on Sunday, the heat of the organ chamber had done its work. No wonder Will Elwell had to come with a hearse and a shovel. Your church is getting quite a reputation for having a hearse parked out front in the parking space." She couldn't help but inject a little levity into the conversation to see how Brownell would react. There was no reaction.

"So now what?" said Brownell.

"Well," continued the Chief, "I'll have to be interviewing some more people from your church. I might even have a stakeout at your worship services and events to watch people. Sometimes more can be found by observing than asking."

"That's alright with me." Said Brownell. "Have as many people as you wish come as observers."

"Where were you last week from Thursday to Sunday? She asked.

"I was in town doing my usual gig. I had Ophelia Peden's funeral earlier in the week. That was quite exhausting. I took some time off and then was in my office mornings preparing for last Sunday."

"How many people have keys to the church?" she asked.

"Too many," said Brownell. "We've tried to limit keys to only 10 people, but some have made copies for their families and others they thought might need a key. It's been a real problem. On more than one occasion I've found doors unlocked overnight. Sometimes lights are left on and heat turned up."

"Have you ever met an Officer Gunnerson?" asked the Chief.

"No, I can't say that I have," answered Brownell. "Why?"

"I just wondered. He stopped in here a couple of days ago. Matter of fact, he was here for Ophelia Peden's funeral. He came to town because he seems to think he saw your red pickup in his town in Maine recently." She said.

"Why would he say that?" asked Brownell.

"He's just covering all his bases because there was a fire in his town, the fire that burned up Ophelia Pedens. He thinks there might be something more to that than just coincidence. He saw a red pickup truck. He jotted down the number plate. He found out it belongs to you, so he came here to investigate."

"Just a coincidence, I suppose." Said Brownell. "I go to Maine several times a year to see a friend. Must have been one of those times when he saw my truck."

"Okay then." Concluded the Chief. "That will be enough for now. I'll be interviewing Otty Bourne and Will Elwell who were both on the scene after worship when I was called on Sunday. I'm sure you have things to do to prepare for Patchy Frost's funeral so until another time, have a good day."

"Thank you for your work," replied Brownell. "I hope that the culprit is found who did this to Patchy. Will the news be out that it was murder?"

"The paper has contacted me and I'll fill them in on the coroner's conclusion." She replied. "I won't give them any details about how it happened or the scene of the crime. I'll just tell them the conclusion is murder and it is under investigation. I'm sorry to bring this news to you. I'm sure it will make it more difficult to deal with the congregation and their grief. May God be with you?"

"Yes," said Brownell, "but it was Patchy that died, not someone like Mercy or Calista. I hope you have a good day."

Rev. Brownell left and in the process with that odd comment, he left Chief more confused and wondering than before. "Why does he not seem very sad that Patchy is dead? She was a thorn in the side of the community even, but…" she thought.

CHAPTER TWENTY FOUR

A GRACE PERCEIVED

"For what partnership is there between righteousness and lawlessness? Or what fellowship is there between light and darkness?" II Corinthians 6:14b, c.

"Day by day, as they spent much time together in the temple, they broke bread at home and ate their food with glad and generous hearts, praising God and having the goodwill of all the people." Acts 2:46-47a

    Mercy hummed as she went about setting up the coffee table. It calmed her nerves and solidified her simple thoughts. *"Amazing Grace, how sweet the sound that saved a wretch like me,"* streamed across her mind's eye as she hummed the tune. She had a tin ear even if she did think that her recent cataract operation on her eyes had improved her hearing. People laughed at her when she'd made that comment during prayer time at worship a few weeks before. Some laughed with her. They knew what she was like, a sweet little old lady who had never married. Harmless. Sometimes helpless. Always helpful.
    "Stop that incessant humming," yelled Barbara Nolan from across the room. She was setting up the table with the silverware and napkins. With Patchy dead and out of the picture, Barbara had taken over. Now she was going to be a thorn in the side of the pastor and an instigator and road block of the church's ministry and mission.
    "Barbara, Barbara," said Calista. "She's not harming anyone. Lighten up." Calista was always the mediator.

Sometimes she was a little Pollyanna, but most of the time she just wanted peace, love and community. "We're here to honor Patchy and to assist one another," she said. "Be gentle."

Barbara gave that glaring look she could give when she was especially angry that her 17 year old daughter had been killed some years before. She said nothing.

Just about then Kallie Jansink came barging through the kitchen door, her arms laden with trays of cold cuts.

"Couldn't one of you hear me knocking at the door," she demanded. "You're all in your little worlds, leaving me standing out there with my arms full. Why are you putting that drink table there and the silverware table way over there? They ought to be next to each other. Move them!" she ordered.

As was usual in many churches, First Church was filled with chiefs, Indians and workers. Too often they had too many chiefs, each who knew exactly what needed to be done, and not enough Indians or workers. A colony of fire ants did a better job of getting along than this group. At least each ant knows their position in life and does their task and stays with it. Not this church group. Kallie Jansink and Barbara Nolan were always ready to clash horns. One would think they were like two bucks during mating season getting ready to battle over a mate.

"Geesh!" Commented Kallie all out of breath and exasperated. "I have all this meat here and you're all just standing around ignoring what has to be done with it. Hey, she continued. "Do you remember the time Audrey's sister Phyllis died in a car accident and we had a funeral for her on a Saturday? We had lots of ham and turkey left over so we put it in the fridge."

"Yeah," said Barbara. "What's your point?"

"The point is," continued Kallie," on Sunday, the day after the funeral, Rev. Brownell got up during the announcements and said, "You all may know that Audrey's sister died this past week. We had the funeral here yesterday.

We had some cold meat left over after and if you'd like some it's in the fridge." Kallie doubled over with laughter.

Calista and Mercy laughed to themselves. Barbara, putting on her queenly newly acquired authority said, "We are not amused. Funny, but not amused."

Kallie set the meat down and went to get a table for the food. She grumbled to herself, "Why weren't these tables all set up before we got here? What's the matter with that sexton? Better yet, what's the matter with that minister?"

Barbara had been thinking the same thing. Mercy, Calista and a few others who had gathered on the tale of the Kallie anecdote went about their business.

"Now that you mention it, Kallie," said Barbara, "some of the things our pastor says ought to be censored. What an awful thing to say after that funeral, "cold meat in the fridge." I know it was a slip of the tongue but.."

"Yeah, slip of the tongue, alright" said Kallie. "He does more than slip over his tongue. It seems to me that he intentionally says one thing and does another. Take for instance last week when we found out about dear Ophelia and had to coordinate a funeral without him. Then he shows up at the last minute, changes our plans and takes over."

"I agree," said Barbara. "What's with that? Where was he anyway? He sure does disappear often without telling anyone where he is going or where he has been. How many times has he been away and was needed and we couldn't find him. I don't even think his wife knows where he is."

"Speaking of his wife," said Kallie now more interested in keeping the conversation going than coordinating the food table. "His wife Eloise sure is a door mat in one way and a social climber in another. I bet she couldn't care less about him. Have you ever seen how they react together? They probably haven't had sex in years, if at all."

"Sex!" said Calista. That had gotten her attention. She had been listening all the time, but had been trying to avoid the mounting controversy. It was turning from mere commentary about the pastor toward a lynching, moral or otherwise. "Sex" she repeated. "How could any of us know anything about that? Girls, Girls, I think you are both beginning to be unkind and getting off the task of why we are here."

"Oh Calista," said Mercy. "They don't mean anything by it. They'll calm down." In truth, Mercy's hearing wasn't as good as she made it out to be. She hadn't heard the worst of it. The worst was yet to come.

Vida Hood arrived carrying her cello. Tom Dougal wasn't far behind. He often came to make sure that the sexton had done his job. Both had come in just in time to overhear the last negative comment.

"What's going on here," said Tom. "I thought we had decided that what happened at the Nolan's stayed at the Nolans."

"What do you mean by that, Tom?" asked Vida.

"Oh nothing much," said Tom as he tried to retreat from the fact he'd let a secret slip out. "We just had a little gathering. It was nothing." He lied.

That didn't' stop Barbara or Kallie. They were bent on character assignation. Barbara was perpetually angry about the death of her daughter years before and she was always taking it out on the congregation or whomever she could target. Kallie, on the other hand, just had a mean know-it-all-want-to-get-my-way streak. Kallie's kids couldn't even stand her. That was evident by how they behaved when they came to worship.

Kallie, Arick and the kids were always properly dressed in go-to-meeting clothes. Not a hair was out of place. Not a wrinkle could be seen. They always looked like they had come out of Family Magazine exemplifying the perfect family. Unfortunately, their outward appearance was a sham. On most Sundays or on occasions such as this fellowship gathering, the real Kallie and Arick would raise its ugly head. Mean was hardly a bad enough word to describe how they related with others in the congregation. They would come across as sweet and cooperative and proper until, until someone crossed the path of their intentions.

Kallie figured Rev. Brownell was ripe for the kicking and she would take every opportunity to kick. Today at the preps for the fellowship time was just as good a time as any. And to top it off, she had an audience.

"Well," said Kallie, "I think it's time we did something about that minister of ours. I think he's nowhere genuine. I don't think he believes a word that comes out of his mouth. Did you hear all that stuff he said about Ophelia at her funeral? Where'd he get that pack of lies? He nowhere knew that much about her than I know about what you did in bed last night. Imagine!"

"I agree," said Barbara. She had heard the conversation at the staff-parish meeting from the night before and she couldn't agree more. "He abuses members. And what about all that money he spends on things we don't need?"

"And" added Kallie, "I've about had my fill of hearing him preach about "Right to Life" and in the same breath preach about LGBT equality and same gender marriage. For all I know he's probably forced his wife to have an abortion or two. Why don't they have any children?"

"If they did have children, they'd be miserable." Said Barbara. "They'd probably be abused, at least verbally."

Vida and Tom had decided to leave the room for other church parts rather than get embroiled in what appeared to be a pastor lynching coming on.

Mercy continued to hum. It was the only way she could maintain her focus on the drink table. Calista silently prayed to herself and considered how she could stop this conversation and calm the waters that were beginning to boil, turning the coffee into bitter mud instead of a fragrant aroma.

What the two, Barbara and Kallie involved in gossip and character assassination didn't know was that Rev. Brownell had started down the hall from the sanctuary to the fellowship hall. He had heard a little of the conversation and stopped just short of entering the room before they ended.

The door to the hallway sung open and in came Rev. Brownell. All conversation stopped as the ladies focused on their organizing the fellowship food.

"Good morning ladies," said Rev. Brownell in his best forced tone of voice. "You're doing such a wonderful job. Patchy would be proud of you coordinating a lovely repast in her memory." He lied. Whatever church members took charge of and arranged, he thought they could always do it better. So compliments from him were rare. Encouragement was rare. Platitudes were frequent.

No one spoke. Each in their own way, however, had thoughts about the day, Patchy and Rev. Brownell. They each probably had their expectations about how the funeral and the day would go.

Mercy continued to hum. *"I once was lost but now am found. T'was blind but now I see."*

CHAPTER TWENTY FIVE

A GRIEF OBSERVED AND CELEBRATED

"There is a way that seems right to a person, but its end is the way to death." Proverbs 14:12

The headline across the day's Loganwood Gazette was,

"WOMAN'S DEATH RULED A MURDER."

"Oh great," murmured Rev. Brownell as he carried the newspaper and his morning coffee from DD into the church. He headed straight for his office to make the final preparations for Patchy Frost's funeral. "This will put an interesting twist to the service." He thought. "People will be thinking more about murder than Patchy. And of course they'll be thinking, murder happened right here in front of them and now the funeral is happening right here."

He had no choice but to buck up his wall, put his myriad of emotions aside and prepare himself to lead a funeral for one of his members that he liked the least.

The hearse was already parked out front indicating that there was some semblance of life happening, if it only to hold funerals. Elwell stood out front in his mourning garb. He rarely wore his tails, but today seemed to be a special occasion. Patchy Frost was getting a send-off worthy of the queen. It was just as she would have orchestrated. The only difference was that she hadn't coordinated the event. Her favorite minister wasn't officiating. She'd outlived Rev. King.

Rev. Brownell was glad that Rev. King was no longer around as well. For years Rev. King, better known as Rex, continually interfered in the life and ministry of First Church. He had moved on to more lucrative and congenial fields where he could work his co-dependency ministry and bring down another church while remaining connected to First Church.

Between Rev. King and Patchy, there was always something brewing. If Patchy wasn't speaking for Rev. Brownell and coordinating his schedule without his approval, Rev. King was contacting members and arranging to do baptisms and weddings. All this was clearly in violation of the laws of the denomination. The denominational hierarchy had warned Rev. King about this intrusion into the life of his former parish. It fell on deaf ears. Even worse, when Rev. King moved on, his wife continued to teach Sunday school at First Church. She stayed connected, ever a reminder of the "beloved" Rev. Rex who had been there for years. The memory of Rev. Rex's years of ministry at First Church preyed upon the current life of the congregation. It was a continual presence hovering over the congregation.

"Now that Patchy is gone," thought Brownell, "and Rev. Rex King is dead, perhaps the congregation can get on with discovering its ministry or just continue the decline started when their beloved Rev. Rex moved on. Thanks to him and Patchy, I've inherited this mess."

Rev. Brownell could never see that some of the difficulties at First Church were of his own making.

Will Elwell had already transferred the casket from the hearse to the sanctuary. Mercy had arrived and was folding bulletins.

Otty was arranging his music as he sat at the organ console. He had managed to pull out the many bent pipes where Patchy had fallen and died. He'd disconnected the wind pressure to that chest of pipes. It was a big organ so he was able to find enough stops on the other manuals that still worked. "It's rather ironic," thought Otty, "I'm going to play the very organ for Patchy's service. Where she died will make beautiful music for celebrate where she's gone." He turned on the organ. The hiss of the air leaking was loud but not unbearable. He would just turn the organ off between musical numbers.

Brownell came down from his office to inspect the scene. Just as the Queen of England inspected the setting and measured everything before a royal banquet, Brownell had to make sure everything was to his liking.

"Does she stink?" he asked Elwell as they stood at the back of the sanctuary. "You have her in one of those cheapo caskets. Does she stink? She sure did last Sunday."

"Nah! She doesn't stink," replied Elwell. "I filled the casket up with some special "shake and bake" embalming powder especially for bodies that have been autopsied. She doesn't stink."

"I'm going to light some incense just the same," said Brownell. "This sanctuary still smells from Sunday. I'm not sure if it smells because she lay dead in that organ chamber, because of that cheap casket today or because there is just plain evil lurking in this building. Evil stinks, you know."

"I've experienced evil and do know that," said Elwell. "Corpses have even spoken to me during the process of preparing them for burial. It's an interesting and sometimes enlightening experience. I had one body some years ago, a man who was murdered way up in Vermont, who actually told me who the murderer was."

Brownell shuddered. "How creepy." He said. "Just what I needed to hear before this funeral. Did Patchy tell you who murdered her?"

"Nah," said Elwell. "She was dead as those bent organ pipes she was lying in. Dead. The organ had had the last word."

People were beginning to arrive for the service so Elwell faded into the background at the back of the sanctuary. He always liked to be present but invisible. One never knew when the funeral director was needed to address any emergency that might happen.

Tom Dougal handed out bulletins. Mercy Haggenmacher attended to the guest book, making sure that each person signed. She didn't know why the funeral director even bothered with a guest book. Patchy didn't have any close relatives who would want it. She figured it probably was an opportunity for Elwell to add another item to the cost of Patchy's funeral.

Brownell was surprised that quite a few people came to the service. "They're either here because they were friends and loved her," he thought, "or they are here to celebrate that she's gone." He walked down the aisle and took his place in the cathedral-like pastor's chair behind the pulpit. The candles were lit. The room was hushed.

The strains of "The Lost Chord," for the second time in a couple of weeks came out of the organ. This time, however, there was no "grand amen" from the organ. Otty was lucky to even find one or two chords to play for the gathering music, no less one lost chord. It worked. Enough of the organ was still playable that it worked.

As the sound of the lost chord that Otty had found died off, Brownell stood and began the service.

"Dear friends," he intoned, "we have gathered here this day to grieve and to celebrate the life of our sister, Patchy Frost. She is a child of God's making. She is a sheep of the fold," he paused thinking to himself, "Even if she was a lost and black sheep." He continued. "She is one of the saints of First Church who now rests from her labors," he paused again. "And," he thought, "From her irritating presence around this place." He continued. "We gather this day to celebrate and rejoice in her life eternal. Amen."

Brownell sat down to listen to Veona Rotowitz sing "Beautiful Isle of Somewhere." "Good to God," he thought, "Is this woman ever going to retire from singing? Her high notes, if she ever had any, are gone and all that's left is a warble like a roto-rooter. In fact, when he spoke to others about Veona, he often referred to her as Veona Roto-rooter. His mind wandered as she sang off to some beautiful isle. He chuckled and cringed at the same time as he listened.

Brownell looked out over the audience. They were as amused and irritated as he. He noticed Chief Blanc had arrived at the last minute, no doubt as a result of the death being ruled a murder. And he noticed another man, the man who had brushed against him when he had gone to the police station. He was relieved that the fellow he'd talked with from DD the day before, Gregg Morrison, wasn't there.

Veona was done singing. Everyone was relieved. The service continued. Scripture readings. The Twenty Third Psalm read by everyone. A Eulogy. This time Brownell had no competition from Patchy. He would do the eulogy and say what he wanted. "The Lord be with you," he said. "And also with you," responded the congregation. *"Let us pray. Almighty God, open our minds and hearts by the power of your Holy Spirit that we might hear and live what you have to say to us today, both from your word and the life of your servant Patchy. Amen."* Brownell paused to gather up his thoughts. Then he began.

"When I think of Patchy I see a Rose. We shall always remember her as the woman with a rose. It was always a big red rose either in her hair or pinned to her dress. She was always color coordinated and well perfumed. She would never be seen in public without the rose somewhere on her person. Of all the people I have known through the years, I have never known anyone like Patchy. You could always see her coming. You could always know that she's been around for she left the scent of her wherever she was or had been. Even her perfume was based on the scent of a rose.

A rose is a beautiful flower. It is one of the most beautiful in the world. It has been cultivated and hybridize. It has been used for centuries as a symbol for love. It has been used as a symbol of mourning. On Mother's day roses are always given out in honor and memory of mothers.

What better to remember Patchy than to remember her with a rose? That is why there is just one rose on the altar today. It is the biggest and most beautiful rose that we could find in Loganwood. To honor her presence with us here in death and to remember her presence with us when she walked among us.

A Rose. They are beautiful. They give off a fragrance. They represent love in all the ways that love is represented and perceived. One of the unique aspects of a rose is that they have thorns. We certainly can identify with a rose that is beautiful and at the same time can prick us and annoy us. Patchy was beautiful. Patchy was loving. Patchy was faithful. Patchy could be thorny and annoying. She was like the rose she always wore. Beautiful but thorny."

The congregation was getting a little nervous. "How far is he going to take this analogy," thought Kallie Jansink. She could identify because even though she didn't wear a rose, she was a lot like Patchy. Beautiful and thorny at the same time. Some others were also getting the gist of the message. "Did he like her?" they thought, "Or is he just being realistic and describing her. He sure is right on." Brownell continued.

Patchy had the unique characteristic of being brutally honest and thorny and beautiful at the same time. It was as if she lived her last name, Frost. Just when you thought the frost was going to descend on the pumpkin, as they say, or the frost was going to thaw, Patchy would put on the deep freeze, stare you down and get you to do whatever it was she wanted you to do. She was the rose, a rose of beauty and a rose of thorns.

So we remember this unique child of God, Patchy Frost. A child of God who graced us with all the varieties of her personality she could muster to bless and annoy and beautify. I close this day with one of the most beautiful songs ever written. Bette Midler penned these words that will live on for eternity. "The Rose"

Some say love, it is a river
That drowns the tender reed.
Some say love, it is a razor
That leaves your soul to bleed.
Some say love, it is a hunger,
An endless aching need.
I say love, it is a flower,
And you its only seed.

It's the heart afraid of breaking
That never learns to dance.
It's the dream afraid of waking
That never takes the chance.
It's the one who won't be taken,
Who cannot seem to give,
And the soul afraid of dyin'
That never learns to live.

When the night has been too lonely
And the road has been too long,
And you think that love is only
For the lucky and the strong,
Just remember in the winter
Far beneath the bitter snows
Lies the seed that with the sun's love
In the spring becomes the rose.

The Rose! Let us pray. O God, whose mercies cannot be numbered: Accept our prayers on behalf of your servant Patchy, and grant her an entrance into the land of light and joy, in the fellowship of your saints; through Jesus Christ our Lord, who lives and reigns with you and the Holy Spirit, one God, now and forever. Amen."

The usual followed: The Apostle's Creed, The Lord's Prayer and a closing hymn, "When the Roll is called up Yonder, I'll be there." As Rev. Brownell led the casket down the aisle and out to the hearse, Otty did as he had planned. He played a medley of hymns. The organ sounded as if it was wheezing its last gasp.

With Patchy safely back in the hearse and Elwell on the way to the cemetery, Brownell disrobed and went to join the congregation in fellowship hall. There were no plans for him or anyone else to attend the lowering of the casket into the grave. What was done was done. It was enough. The rose had faded and was buried.

CHAPTER TWENTY SIX

THE ESCAPE

Brownell breathed a sigh of relief. "Thank goodness that's over with." He whispered. "And I'm done with that nosey Patchy as well. Good riddance. I never thought I'd be free of her incessant meddling." He made his way down the hallway to the fellowship hall, relieved that most had left by the front door. Only a few close friends of Patchy and regular church members had stayed on.

"They'll always come for food," he said as he passed Mercy pouring coffee at the beverage table. "I bet that'll get in the Loganwood Gazette. MERCEDES HAGGENMACHER POURED AT THE FUNERAL OF PATCHY FROST." Silly people. They'll do anything to be recognized.

There were quite a few people mingling around. He could see that they had formed into little clusters. He had no desire to join any of the little gatherings. He could just imagine what their conversation was like. The conversations before, during and after funerals just drove him insane. They were so trite and meaningless. He had heard people say "I know just how you feel," so often that he wanted to punch someone, or at least shake them into some kind of sanity. No one knows how another person feels. That's the most insensitive thing anyone could say. Just wait till they experience some trauma, maybe then they'll stop saying that kind of drivel.

He made his rounds of the people gathered, making sure that they had seen him. When no one was looking, Brownell slipped down the hallway to his office where he quickly changed out of his clergy clothes and into some jeans and a tee shirt. There was a private entrance to his office into the side alley. He only used it on occasions such as this when he wanted to make a quick getaway.

He headed for the Dunkin Donuts down the street where he could relax, have coffee and a sugar rush.

"Hello, Rev. Brownell" said Addy Teachout, the pleasant woman who worked afternoons. "What can I get you today?"

"A large coffee black and one of those lemon filled donuts, please." He said. "I'll sit at the counter today. Looks like it's a quiet afternoon."

"Yes," she said. "It's been pretty quiet. Not too much traffic in the afternoon. People have either settled in to their afternoon nap, or have their nose to the grindstone before going home. You usually don't come in this late. What brings you in this afternoon?"

"I just finished a funeral. Glad to have a little space to relax before I go home to my wife." He rolled his eyes as if to say "so much for peace when I get home."

"Things not too good at home?" asked Addy.

"Could be better." He let his guard down. There was no one else in the shop to hear. He had known Addy ever since he had moved Loganwood. She was a good woman and he thought he could trust her. "The wife isn't much interested in me or anything I do. She doesn't even act like a wife."

"That's too bad," said Addy. "It happens to the best of us. We either hang in there or we split. Me? I chose to split years ago. Enough with that verbal and physical abuse. I'd rather work here for peanuts than get bounced around by some clod."

"That's too bad," said Brownell. "By the way, I noticed, every time I've been in here lately, that truck with Maine number plates has been sitting out front. Who's it belong to?"

"Not sure." She replied. "Some young fellow who had been hanging around here. Haven't seen him in a day or two.

Probably hooked up with some dame and found her more interesting than the truck. Go figure. You never know what's going to happen at a DD." She laughed.

"Hmmm." Said Brownell. "Did you know Patchy Frost?"

"Just to recognize her if I saw her. Didn't know her personally," she said. "Darn shame what happened to her. And you did the funeral."

"What do you mean?" asked Brownell.

"Murdered," she replied. "You know. Didn't you see the paper this morning? Big headlines. "Woman's death ruled a murder." Now who would do something like that?

"One never knows," he replied. "You know, being in this minister business I've seen and heard it all. I even heard a church member one day say "if you hurt my best friend, I can make your death look like an accident." I wouldn't put it past anyone doing anything. I did see the headline earlier but I was so involved in Patchy's funeral I had to put it aside for the moment. Now that I think about it, it was quite odd officiating at one of my church members who was murdered in the very room where we were holding her funeral."

Addy shivered. "That does give me the creeps. What a weird situation. You have to talk about the dead person right in front of her. Well, I mean right where the person was murdered."

Brownell sipped his coffee. He had already eaten the lemon donut covered in powdered sugar. Now he was covered in powdered sugar. At least his tee shirt was white and the sugar didn't show much.

"So that truck's been here for a couple of days?" he asked, making small talk.

"Yeah," replied Addy. "I suppose I ought to have it towed off or call the cops. Maybe the guy will show up sooner or later. Odd sort of chap, he was." She continued. "He spent a lot of time just sitting here sipping coffee and staring at the people coming in and out. Didn't cause any trouble, but just acted rather, well, imbecilic. Like there was something wrong with him. Like he was on a mission. Like he was out wanting to hook up with someone."

"Oh well." Said Brownell. "The world is full of kooks. Who knows? We may be kookier than everyone else. Then again, I do know that as far as you and I go, neither of us is kooky, but sometimes I wonder about you." He gave out a big belly laugh.

Fortunately Addy had a sense of humor and got the joke. They laughed together. It lightened the tedium of the afternoon.

CHAPTER TWENTY SEVEN

PILLOW TALK

"Do you want to?" said Brownell as he crawled into his side of the king size bed. The bed was so big that if anything were to happen in the bedroom between Lee and Eloise, one or the other would have to make a great effort to make it happen. The space between them was never-never land. The passion that each had for the other had long gone, died out. Their relationship was like the old parable pastors told about the ember that is taken out of the fire and allowed to linger on the hearth. It soon grows cold.

Eloise's and Lee's "ember" had grown cold long ago. Not even Viagra could help Lee get excited about Eloise. The only thing that excited Eloise was some new friend in uppity society or a new position in some high-snot city or country organization that would get her somewhere.

Eloise was well known in upper class circles. She was friends with people like the Secretary of State whose wife was president of the National Garden Club. Eloise was the Garden Club secretary. She often stayed at the homes of the owners of the Boston Globe, the American Heritage Society and the president of the Daughters of the American Revolution. Eloise had an easy in with the DAR group since her maiden name was Choate and everyone knows the Choate name. They even founded a high-snot private school in Connecticut. Best of all, Eloise was a member of the Colonial Dames of New England. She could trace her heritage back to the Mayflower. Eloise thought marrying Brownell would get her an open door to some more upper middle class clubs. First

Church, after all, had been THE church where people of any means or social standing went in Loganville. Those attending there now, however, hadn't noticed that times had changed and First Church was becoming just a fortress shell of a building with empty people with empty heads and cold hearts.

That didn't bother Eloise. She'd try anyway. She often joked that she was going to write a book entitled, "Sleeping Around with Eloise Choate." It was going to be a guide to all of the guest rooms she'd slept in the homes of the rich and famous. She never wrote the book.

"So," said Lee. "How about it?"

"How about what?" said Eloise.

"How about fulfilling your wifely duties and helping me relax after a stress-filled day."

"Ha!" said Eloise, as she rolled over.

Lee rolled over toward here, closing the divide in the big king size bed.

"I have a headache." Murmured Eloise from under the covers she'd pulled up over her head.

Lee spooned her.

"Get that thing away from me," said Eloise. "After hearing what you had to say about Patchy Frost today, I just want to gag every time I see you."

"What do you mean?" said Lee.

"I mean," replied Eloise, "that was nothing but a pack of lies. You couldn't stand her. And then you go and say all that crap about her. The rose and all."

"Well," replied Lee, "Everyone deserves to have a good funeral no matter how evil or bad they were."

"I can't stand funerals where all this good crap is told about a person when it's not true." Replied Eloise. "I didn't particularly like Patchy but she didn't need to be made into a saint." She rolled closer to the edge of the bed. "I said," shouted Eloise, "get that thing away from me."

Lee rolled over on his back. It was no use. Not even his wife gave him the time of the day. The only thing he was good for was a roof over her head, a status in society, and his health insurance.

"Did you read the paper this morning?" Eloise asked, having turned over to look at Lee.

"Yes. What of it?" he replied.

"WOMAN'S DEATH RULED A MURDER!" That's what of it," she yelled. "How could you do that funeral service and not make one mention of the reality of the situation. How could you not make one ounce of effort to try to console the people sitting there who had also just read those headlines. YOU BASTARD," she yelled through tears streaming down her face. "You don't care a twit. All you care about is yourself and your god holy time away, and money, and, and..." she rolled with her back toward him.

"and that I rarely get any satisfaction from my wife," he whispered, as he rolled his back toward her, hunkered down and tried to find some sleep.

CHAPTER TWENTY EIGHT

A BOURNE MOMENT

Now that Patchy Frost's death was ruled a murder, Chief Blanc set out to interview as many people as possible who might know something. Since Otty Bourne discovered the body in the organ chamber on Sunday morning last, it only made sense that she call him down to her office. He wasn't a suspect, but he was a person of interest.

"Mr. Bourne," said the Chief. "How long have you been the organist at First Church?"

"For around 12 years," he replied.

"So you have been here for quite some time. She continued. "During your twelve years at First Church you must have observed lots of people and their interactions with each other."

"Indeed!" he said, "Working at a church is like any organization. There are those who you like and some you don't. There's always some drama going on. I prefer just to do my job. I have enough drama at home with my wife."

"How so?" asked the Chief.

"Vida?" he continued. "Vida, Vida, Vida. Poor Vida. We had a great marriage at first but as the years went on she became less interested in me and more interested in that damn cello of hers. She's more often than not off doing a gig and leaving me to fend for myself."

"I'm sorry to hear that," replied the Chief. "But that doesn't really have anything to do with Patchy's death, does it?"

"Not at all," said Otty. "It's just a fact of life, I guess. Happens to the best of them. I've had couples in my choir who've been married for years and then given up. Just recently I had a couple who'd been married for 40 years. She wanted to own a bed and breakfast so they bought one. It was OK for a while until the husband got fed up with dealing with his wife and the guests. He got a divorce."

"That kind of thing will put stress on a marriage." Said the Chief. "Have you noticed anything unusual going on in the congregation lately?"

"Nothing that hasn't been going on for some time." He replied. "The pastor has his marital problems with a wife who is just interested in social climbing. Patchy had her problems,"

"Patchy?" asked the Chief. "What do you mean?"

"Oh," continued Otty, "she could be a real pain in the ass. You could see her coming from a distance with her big red rose in her hair or pinned to her loud-color dress. And then there was that perfume she wore. It laid down a smoke screen wherever she was or was headed for. Buyer beware! Here comes Patchy!"

"And?" asked the Chief.

"And you'd better be ready for her." He said. "You never knew if she was going to be complimentary or belligerent. If it was the latter it was always because she had some opinion about something or someone or she wanted something. And if she wanted something, it often had no rhyme or reason. She just wanted her way. It was her way or the highway."

"So she wasn't the most liked person in the congregation?" asked the Chief.

"No she wasn't." continued Otty, "but to be generous about her, I do have to say, she had a good heart and did a lot of good for the church. Why, sometimes if it weren't for Patchy, the church would have caved in."

"Really? So she was hated, liked and needed at the same time?" said the Chief.

"Exactly." Replied Otty. "Whenever you needed something done and done right, you could depend upon her. Just as long as you could put up with her obsessive, compulsive behavior. She was a perfectionist. Even though people didn't much like or care for her, they would still ask her to do for them and the church. They would especially ask her to do what they didn't want to do."

"Like?" asked the Chief.

"Like make a last minute run to the grocery to get something that was needed. She'd call you a dunce for not planning ahead, but she'd go ahead and do the errand." Said Otty. "One Easter when we were having an Easter Breakfast between services I watched her in the kitchen. Onie, one of our very elder members was making pancakes. She'd flip them over and then whop them with the spatula."

"That would kill the pancakes," said the Chief.

"Yeah!" Otty laughed. "When Patchy had seen enough of this pancake flattening, she grabbed the spatula out of Onie's hand and said, "STOP DOING THAT. YOU'RE FLATTENING THEM OUT. GIVE ME THAT! I'LL DO IT."

"So she was a take-charge, my way or the highway type of church member?" Said the Chief.

"You got it!" replied Otty.

"You were the first one to find Patchy, correct?" asked the Chief.

"Yes." Said Otty.

"What was your first impression? How did it happen that you found her?" asked the Chief.

"When I first saw her I didn't know whether to gag, throw up or celebrate!" said Otty. "Then I began to think about the horrible scene we'd have if the congregation showed up in 45 minutes and the sanctuary was full of police, funeral directors and god knows who else."

"What did you do?" Asked the Chief.

"I went to Rev. Brownell's office. He was already at the church when I arrived to practice the organ. That's how I knew something was wrong. When I turned the organ on and started to play, a whole section of the organ wheezed and didn't play." Said Otty. "Anyway, I went to Brownell and told him what I'd found. He came down and looked too."

"And what kind of reaction did he have?"asked the Chief.

"Oh, he was pretty disturbed too." Said Otty. "He kept saying "What are we going to do? The congregation will be here shortly." That's when we both decided it was best to wait until after the worship service to deal."

"So you both agreed?" asked the Chief.

"Yes." Said Otty. "We thought it best not to put the congregation in an uproar. That would happen on its own timing when the word got out about Patchy's death. We didn't need to feed the fire. Besides, worship seemed more important than a dead body and chaos at the time."

"So you left her there behind the organ case, just as I saw her after you'd called me?" asked the Chief. The chief thought that was kind of a weird tactic. Most people would rush to call the police. In some ways it was kind of Brownell and Otty to not tell the congregation before or during the worship service. In another way it was pretty macabre of them to know that they and a whole group of people were worshiping God while Patchy lay there, all bloated and purple making her way to heaven or hell, a red rose in her hair and eyes staring at the ceiling.

The chief shivered. She didn't let Otty see, however, that this murder scene was one that just sent chills up and down her spine. "What, do you suppose, she was doing in the organ chamber?" asked the Chief.

"There's altar hangings on a clothes rack near the pipes." Said Otty. "I just supposed that she had come into the church as she so often did, to attend to the altar for the coming Sunday. It did appear that she had been reaching for the hangings. It didn't occur to me that she'd been murdered. I just thought she must have lost her footing, tripped and fell head first into the pipes. Sure destroyed that part of the organ. It's going to cost a ton of money to repair. What a mess."

"Well," said the Chief, "As you know from the newspaper, her death has been ruled a homicide. Someone was in to get her. Do you have any clue as to who might have done this?"

"Wasn't me!" blurted out Otty.

"I don't suspect it was you." Said the Chief. "But I did have to interview you. It sounds like the murderer could have been just about anyone."

"That's true," said Otty with a sigh of relief. "Patchy had lots of enemies. Well, at least, let's say, Patchy had many people who steered clear of her or just plain didn't like her. Her only real friend was Ophelia Pedens. Too bad she got burned up in a fire. We buried her last week! That left Patchy with no-one to moderate her behavior."

"We are aware of Ophelia Peden's death." Said the Chief. "It's been brought to our attention by the authorities in Maine."

That surprised Otty. He'd thought Ophelia was just a victim of circumstances, at the wrong place at the wrong time. "I liked Ophelia," commented Otty.

"Thank you for coming on down." Replied the Chief. "You've been very helpful. I know where to find you should we need to talk again. Probably at the wheezing pipe organ, right?" she chuckled. Chief Blanc wasn't above a laugh now and then.

"Yeah! Right!" said Otty as he got up to leave. "Wheezing for sure. The organ and maybe me too."

CHAPTER TWENTY NINE

A GRIEF REVIEWED

As soon as Rev. Brownell had skipped out of the fellowship time after Patchy's funeral, the volume of the conversation in fellowship hall began to escalate. One could hear snippets of conversations here and there that ranged from appreciation to the funeral to indignation over what Rev. Brownell had said about Patchy.

"I told you he wouldn't hang around," said Kallie Jansink. She was delighted that Rev. Brownell had skipped out. It was one more prediction confirmed. She thought all along that he wasn't much interested in the people of the church. "He ran out of here as if he were going to a fire. Did you notice?"

"I did," replied Barbara Nolan. She and Kallie were somewhat in cahoots most of the time. The rest of the time they were in contention for winning the Oscar for "Most-Difficult-Church Member."

Kallie always wanted everything just so. It was her way or the highway. She wasn't the one who willingly took the highway. She'd rather fight than switch. She was a fighter for what she thought was right, even when it was wrong.

Barbara Nolan wanted everything her way, but for reasons other than to control. Barbara did anything she could to take the focus off of her grief. Anything that would justify the death of her daughter some years before in a car accident, Barbara would do. She would fill up her church time just to run the other way from her grief. She would take on a project thinking it would atone for her sin of parental neglect. That's how she perceived her involvement in the fatal car accident of her daughter. It was her parental neglect that caused the accident. Nothing could be further from the truth, but that didn't matter to Barbara. She tried everything to rid herself of the past. Still the past defined her present and caused her to try to define the present of everyone else around her.

Rev. Brownell was so fed up with Kallie that upon one occasion he even told her that her behavior was bullshit. Of course that just made matters worse. She wrote that down as part of her ammunition to make his life miserable.

As for Barbara Nolan, Rev. Brownell was sick and tired of the old swan song. One day he suggested she get a new violin and play it to another crowd. "I've already heard that side of the record and have it memorized," he said. "How about flipping the record over and playing another song." Barbara wasn't capable of doing that. Her record of life was stuck in her daughter's grave groove.

Tom Dougal overheard the conversation between Barbara and Kallie. He drifted over to join in. Arick Jansick and Dudley Nolan gathered into the group. In short order there were at least ten people standing around with coffee in their hands and venom in their hearts.

Even the members of the congregation who were usually considerate and forgiving stood on the fringe of what appeared to be a mounting mutiny. Some even spoke in those terms.

"Our ship is sinking," said Arick Jansick. "What are we going to do about it?"

"What do you mean?" said Esther Howlane.

"Our pastor," continued Arick, "is incompetent. He's bringing us down. We're becoming the laugh stock of Loganwood. How many times, lately, have you seen Will Elwood and his 1958 Cadillac Hearse parked out front of our church?"

"Twice," replied Tom Dougal. "Once at Ophelia's funeral. Today at Patchy's funeral."

"Exactly," said Kallie. "And who is going to be next? You know these things come in threes. Maybe it'll be one of us. Maybe it'll be our pastor. Maybe we ought to make sure that the next "funeral" around here is our pastor riding out of town in his red pickup truck," she continued, "or in a hearse" she whispered.

Several overheard that comment. Mercy, usually not to say too much, spoke up. "You don't mean that. That's a very unkind thing to say. Pastor tries his best."

"You always find something good in everyone," replied Kallie. "Even in Brownell" she continued with a determined and disgusted tone.

"I do," said Mercy. "Everyone needs the benefit of the doubt. None of us is immune to sin."

"But," continued Barbara, "Some are not immune. Some instead embrace sin."

Dudley Nolan spoke up. "We talked about some of this the other night. It sounds now like panic is setting in. Either we do something or we resign ourselves to waiting it out. Pastor's don't stay forever."

"Neither do church members," said Elaine Howlane. "I can name at least 90 who have left this church since Brownell arrived."

"Maybe once he's gone lots of people will come back." Said Arick.

"Well that's a nice thought" said Calista who had been standing on the fringe sipping her coffee and considering the tone of the gathering. "You know," she said, "many of those people who left, left feet first. They died. What do you think they are going to do? Come back from the grave?"

Some were "not amused" with Calista's reality check. Others agreed with her. Most continued to make a list of all those families and singles who had left because of Rev. Brownell.

"When you come right down to it," said Tom Dougal, "our church is pretty split over a number of issues. If it isn't our disappointment over our minister, it's our disgust with the politics of the country, or it's the divisions that are occurring over the radical right-wing conservative positions our denomination is taking. We can't blame it all on Brownell."

"YES WE CAN!" shouted Kallie. She was sure that she knew the cause of their church divisions. "Get those damn "welcome-everyone-people" out of our denomination and our church and things will be lots better. We want only people who are like us. If everyone would be NICE LIKE ME things would just be wonderful."

That caused some eyes to cross in the group. But not one in the group had the grit to tell Kallie that she was full of Bullshit. The pastor had already done that and it hadn't worked. It had only made her more determined to spread her bullshit around. Patchy's funeral was a great opportunity. And on top of it all, the fact that the morning paper had ruled Patchy's death a homicide, gave Kallie even more incentive to stir the dirt up from the bottom of the pot.

"What did you make of this morning's headlines?" asked Kallie. "Didn't you think it was rather odd that Otty the organist and our Pastor let us go on and worship while that rotting corpse was on the other side of the organ case. Sometimes it is better not knowing what is what but in this case…" She paused with a disgusted look on her face.

Someone in the unofficial lynch-the-pastor group commented. "I agree." Someone else said, "It was despicable that we were kept in the dark. We were treated like children."

"Exactly," said Barbara. "And to top it all off, what did you think of that eulogy this afternoon? "The Rose." Everyone knows how much Brownell hated Patchy. And everyone knows how much Patchy was out to continually goad Brownell. She was in his face all the time." Barbara paused as if to consider what she had just said. "Well," she continued, "she was in our face all the time too but at least most of us treated her with respect. We didn't' always cow to her wishes but..."

"I think," said Arick, "that the eulogy today was ingenuous. Of course everyone knows the kind of relationship he had with Patchy and she with him. Then for him to get up there and talk all about roses, and light and love. What a pack of lies."

"I think dead people always deserve the best," said Mercy. She would say that. She always thought the best of others, even if they were the worst. "Everyone ought to have some good things said about them after they're dead." She paused, "or after they have left the church, town or the country, for that matter."

In the instance of Patchy's eulogy, most couldn't disagree more. Most thought that it might have been safer for Rev. Brownell to just ask people to share memories. People always think of funny and positive things to say. By the people sharing, the pressure is off the minister to tell lies. Some just thought a service no eulogy at all would have been just fine. And they would have gotten out of church and to the fellowship food sooner. They laughed.

"Well," said Dudley, "you probably all know that you're talking to the chairperson of the staff-parish committee. There are also some members of that committee here. I think we've got some major issues to discuss, other than the gossip that is going around this room and this town about our pastor. Our congregation is ignorant but it's not all their fault. Sure, they are lazy about participating, reading and knowing what their church is doing but," he paused, "we are also guilty of allowing our pastor to get away with what I'd call mis-management or abuse of members, financial irresponsibility, and lack of accountability. Right now he's off somewhere. We know not where. He could be on a jaunt for a couple of days for all we know. He's done it before. He'll do it again. And while he's off on a toot, we have a crisis and administration that goes wanting."

The volume in the group began to escalate again. It was bordering on becoming a riot right there in fellowship hall. It was obvious the church was going down, losing its influence in the community and becoming the laughing stock of Loganwood.

"He asks me to sing at funerals a lot," whimpered Veona Rotowitz.

"BIG DEAL!" said Kallie. "Your singing days ought to be over. Your warble is warbled out. You sound more like Roto-rooter than a nightingale."

"That's not funny,"said Elaine Howlane as Veona began to cry."

"I just want to offer my best gift to God," said Veona through the tears streaming down her elderly face.

"Your gift needs a new wrapping," said Kallie without missing a beat.

"That's even less funny," said Elaine. "If you can't say something good about someone, then keep your mouth shut. Better yet, if you insist on being stupid, at least have enough sense to not say anything and confirm your stupidity."

Elaine rarely came up against anyone, no less someone like Kallie. This time Kallie had found where Elaine's goat was tied. Elaine saw through Kallie like looking through a freshly washed windshield in broad daylight. Elaine wasn't going to have any of it.

For once Kallie shut up. Elaine took the stage and forcefully engaged in the debate. "I think it's time that each of us stuffed a donut in our mouths and stifled. The way this conversation has gone, we've lowered ourselves to something less than Christian. So much for "see how they love each other." Anyone coming in here just now would be out the door in a flash. We've satisfied ourselves. We know each of us is not alone in our thinking. We know there are ways to deal with issues such as this. So let's tamp down this rhetoric and let our staff-parish work through our concerns."

"I agree," said most, one after another.

"We'll be having a meeting shortly. I assure you, we'll address the issues you have raised. Now, "said Dudley, "no matter what you thought of the funeral, or Patchy or even Brownell, let's honor the reason we gather as people of God. Let's honor one another and love as Jesus would love."

Silence fell upon the group. In a not so gentle way they had revealed their hearts. In a gentle way they had been reminded of why they gather and how they ought to be with each other.

"I think," said Dudley, "it would serve us well if we'd form a circle, hold hands and take a moment."

By this time there was about 20 people in on the conflab. Most obeyed and formed a circle. Kallie refused to stay. She and her husband Arick stormed out. As usual, they had to leave making a scene.

The group held hands and looked to Dudley to lead them. "I suggest," said Dudley, "that we take a moment of silence. Take a deep breath. Then before any words are spoken, let us each in our own way, look at each person in this circle. I remind you that we are all children of God."

Quiet. In what seemed to be five minutes, one could hear the breathing around the circle work to breathing in unison. The group gradually moved toward being one in heart.

"Let us pray," said Dudley. *"Creator God, we pray for our church. We pray for each person in this circle. We pray for those not here, for those outside this circle. We pray,"* he paused, *"for our pastor. We sometimes lose our way. We sin and forget to ask for forgiveness. We judge others when it is we ourselves who ought to be judged. Walk with us in these days of anguish. Enable us to understand and failing to understand, empower us to accept what is and become all that you would have us be. Thank you. Amen."*

"Let us make merry and be glad, for today, Patchy sees the Kingdom of Heaven, I think," said Otty's wife, Vida Hood. She chuckled and headed for the cheese. She was always more about partying than anything else anyway.

CHAPTER THIRTY

DEATH SPEAKS

Ever since Will Elwell picked up the body of Patchy Frost and arranged her parts on his embalming table he had an uneasy feeling about the whole scene.

He was the third person to arrive at the scene after Otty Bourne and Rev. Brownell. It was not an uncommon scene other than it happened in a church and in a pipe organ chamber. Patchy was sprawled out in such a way that he was suspicious.

"How could someone fall into organ pipes, get knocked out and die?" thought Elwell. He chose not to say anything. He went about his business of removing the body, transporting it and preparing it for burial.

Having been in the funeral business for decades, Elwell had seen it all. He had also heard it all. He'd heard relatives say strange and mysterious things about their deceased loved ones. He'd heard so much from the living about the dead that upon occasion and out of curiosity he had asked survivors if they had seen or experienced their loved one after they had departed.

About a year prior to Patchy's death, Elwell had handled the funeral of a thirty nine year old woman. She had died of cancer. As he was visiting with the husband of the deceased, Elwell asked, "Arnold, have you seen your wife, Tamara?"

Arnold paused and thought for a moment and seeing that Elwell's office at the funeral home was a safe place, he replied, "Yes. I saw her outside of our house on the lawn."

"Well, I must tell you, Arnold," offered Elwell, "That when I was preparing Tamara for burial I experienced a very strong perfume that filled the embalming room. I don't like perfume so I noticed it immediately. I have nothing more to think than it was Tamara present with me as I prepared her body."

Elwell remembered that Arnold was comforted by the knowledge that someone else had experienced his deceased wife. Persons don't often share such intimate experiences out of fear or rejection. Elwell's openness to the possibility of the presence of the deceased being around, provided a safe haven and opportunity for others to tell their stories.

The most disturbing time for Elwell was when he experienced the deceased stretched out on the embalming table. On more than one occasion the deceased had spoken to him revealing all sorts of information about their life and their experience of death.

So, when Patchy Frost, all stretched out on Elwell's table with no place to go began to speak to him, he was startled.

Before the headlines of Patchy's death being ruled a murder ever hit the Loganwood Gazette, Will Elwell already knew that she had been murdered. He had seen the dent on the back of her head where she'd been struck by something. That was his first clue.

He was most startled when Patchy began to speak to him about her demise. "She'd been looking in the organ chamber for hangings to dress the altar for the coming Sunday," she said.

Elwell listened carefully. "It was dark," said Patchy. "It was very dark but I could see the hangings on the rack near the pipes. It was early evening and I was alone in the church. As I reached for the hanging I was looking for, I heard the door creak behind me. Before I could turn around something hit me on the back of the head and I fell into the pipes. That was it."

Elwell stood up straight. He had been bending over Patchy's body. A shudder went through his spine. "It was murder," he whispered to himself. "Does she know who it was?"

A cold quiet descended over the room, the kind when evil lurks in every corner of a place. There was no need for evil to be there, other than to stop Patchy from telling who it was that killed her, if she even knew. Evil had already been done.

Elwell waited. There was nothing but silence. Dare he ask the question, "Who did it?" Did he really want to know? And if he did find out, what would he do with the information?

He stood there in the sterile silence of the sterile room. Just he and the corpse.

"Who did it?" he whispered.

Silence.

Then a chill as cold as the ice on the river in winter.

Then a warmth.

He knew.

CHAPTER THIRTY ONE

COFFEE AND ---

Addy Teachout was on duty at Dunkin Donuts the morning after Patchy Frost's funeral. It was one of those grey autumn days that can descend upon New England. It is neither autumn nor winter but it definitely announces that something is about to happen. There had been way too much going on in Loganwood to suit Addy but there was nothing she could do about it. The best she could do was put on her usual happy face and attend to her coffee brewing and customers.

"Good Morning. Welcome to Dunkin Donuts," she said as Officer Gunnerson approached the counter. "May I help you?"

"I'll have a double-double please," he replied.

"A double-double?" she asked with a confused look.

"Oh! I'm sorry," he said. "I'm from Downeast Maine. We have Tim Horton donuts shops there. There's lots of Canadians that come over the border and that's how they order their coffee."

"I see." She said as she gave out a little chuckle. "What's it mean."

"It means two sugars, two creams. Some people even ask for "triple-triple." I guess it's the lazy way of ordering." He translated his order into Dunkin Donut speak. "I'll have a large coffee with two sugars and two creams, please."

"Would you like anything else?" she asked.

"Yes," he replied as he scanned the large donut rack behind her. "I'll take one of those Boston creams. I'm in the

Boston area. Ought to have a donut that is named for the place. And I'll take one of those maple frosted."

He looked to see if there was space in the seating area. For some odd reason, there weren't many customers right at the moment so he eyed where he would sit. He paid and collected his order.

"Are you here most mornings?" asked Gunnerson.

"I rotate shifts." Replied Addy. Sometimes I'm here in the afternoon. Lately, I've been here most mornings. Is there something I can help you with? Although he wasn't wearing a uniform, she had noticed his badge when he had opened his wallet. "You're from Maine? I noticed your car number plate."

"Yes." He said. "It's the first time I've been to this area. Came down for a reason. If you have time, I'd like to chat a little. I'll take a seat and wait to see if you have a moment. Come over and join me."

"It will be my time for a break shortly." She said. "One of the other girls can take over at the register. I'll come over in a few."

"Great." He said as he headed for a table.

It wasn't long before Addy joined him. She brought her coffee and an extra donut for him. "I thought you might like this. It's our autumn selection. Pumpkin spice."

"That's very nice of you. Thank you." Replied Gunnerson. "I just have a couple of questions that you might be helpful with."

"I'll try," she said.

"You see many people during the day here." He began. "I imagine you have regular customers and then you have people passing through. I'm in town because we've had a murder where I'm from."

"Where is that?" asked Addy.

"Somewhere, Maine." He replied. "It's a little nothing of a place that with the recent uproar has made a name for itself and has been in the news. You may have read about us in your local paper. Do you remember reading about one of your local people burning up in a fire?"

"I do." She replied. "I think they just had a funeral for her."

"Yes," he continued. "Ophelia Pedens. I attended the funeral."

"Did you know her?" She asked.

"I knew her only because she was the one who discovered the murdered man in our church. She called me and that started the investigation. She never knew who committed the murder but..."

"Did you solve the murder?" she leaned in and asked in a whisper.

"Sure did," he continued. "But not because of Ophelia. The murderers did themselves in. That often happens. People revisit the scene of the crime. Three people did the murder. They all were convicted. Two got jail time and one got house arrest and many years of probation. Clipped their wings, I'll tell ya." He said with satisfaction.

"I'll bet." She replied. "I wouldn't want to be in their shoes. Or in the shoes of the victim for that matter. So why are you here if the murder was solved?"

"Because," he said, "I'm not convinced that Ophelia Pedens just happened to get burned up in that fire. I suspect she was murdered. My bet is there was some good reason for ending her days."

"Really?" she asked in amazement. "And you think it might have something to do with Loganwood other than she was from here? Maybe someone from here wanted her gone?"

"Exactly," he answered. "I think Ophelia's death has a lot to do with Loganwood and not much to do with Somewhere Maine. So let me ask you some questions, Okay?"

"Sure." She agreed. "Anything I can do to help." This was turning out to be one of the most exciting days of her work week. Usually her days were routine. Coffee, donuts and cash. Now she was offered intrigue to go along with the customer's order. "Ask away."

"I notice that for a couple of days there was a truck parked out front with Maine number plates. Do you know who it belonged to?"

"I think it belonged to a fellow who came in for a few days and would just sit and stare at the customers." She answered. "He was rather odd fellow. He didn't bother anyone but he seemed to be quite interested in who came and went." She paused. "We noticed that a couple of days ago he stopped coming in but that truck was still out there. We finally had it towed away to the impound yard. It was making parking difficult for our regular customers."

"And you haven't seen him since?" asked Gunnerson.

"No." she replied. "Was that his truck?"

"I think so." He answered. "I was about to check the number plate but then it was gone. I can find it at the impound yard, I'm sure. My thinking is that it belongs to one of the people convicted in the church murder down home. If it does belong to the young fellow who got house arrest, then I'll get a warrant to arrest him. He's in violation of his parole."

"He's in trouble for sure." He replied. "His first mistake was to hang with the little clique in our town that committed the murder. Aside from that he's a pervert. Not a pedophile. Just a pervert who likes to stalk men in the hopes that he'll get in their pants. He's a real sicko."

"Ick!" groaned Addy. "And? There's more?"

"It doesn't have anything to do with Loganwood or you or this DD shop but the oddest thing about him is that he used to hide in the steeple of our church. He had found a body board up there. He'd strip naked, lie on it, and fantasize who had been dead and used the board. He especially liked to do that when the congregation was present down in the sanctuary."

Addy gasped.

"Thankfully," Gunnerson continued, "With the murder shenanigans the three and the congregation engaged in, the church was closed and boarded up never to see a congregation again. He can't hang in the steeple anymore. Evidently, he has other interests."

"I don't understand." She commented.

"Well, since he is under house arrest, he's exhausted his opportunities for excitement. No more hanging out in the woods in wait for a trick to pass by."

"So," she asked, "what's that got to do with Loganwood?"

"I went to his house up in the woods several weeks ago," he continued, "because I had noticed a man with Massachusetts number plates driving around our town. I wrote down his number when we were in the thick of investigating the murder and the fire. It turns out the truck belongs to Rev. Brownell."

Addy gasped. She was quite familiar with Rev. Brownell. "He often comes in here," she commented. "This is one of his places to hang out when he needs a break."

"I asked this young fellow," he paused. "His name is Gregg, by the way. I asked him if he knew anything about Rev. Brownell. All he knew was that he'd seen this man cruising through the woods by a pull-off in our town. He assumed that he was there for the same reason.. He didn't know who the man was until I told him. I assumed it was Rev. Brownell since that's who the number plate was registered to."

"Ah!" she exclaimed. "And you think that there's a connection here to our town?"

"Yes!" he continued. "If it has anything to do with Ophelia burning up in the fire, I'm not sure. If the man in the red pickup was in fact, Rev. Brownell, then it seems rather odd that Ophelia and he would be in the same town in Maine at the same time. I think…"

Addy finished his sentence. "You think that Rev. Brownell has something to do with Ophelia's death? Or?"

"Or it was just happenstance." He continued. "I think Rev. Brownell was in our town to satisfy his gay, or at least bisexual urges. I think Ophelia and Brownell recognized each other. Ophelia, I think, would have come back to Loganwood and blown his cover and that would have been the beginning of the end of his career."

Addy sat in stunned silence. "Where's this Gregg guy now?" she asked.

"I don't know." He replied. "It seems he's disappeared if in fact, that was his truck that got towed. You haven't seen him lately?"

"No," she answered. "It can be quite busy in here. I don't always notice who is here and who is missing."

"And," continued Gunnerson, "What do you know about Rev. Brownell?"

"He comes in here quite often. Matter of fact he was in here after Patchy Frost's funeral." She paused. "Wasn't that a shame?"

"How do you mean?" he asked.

"I mean, murder and all. She wasn't much liked around town but still, no one deserves to be murdered."

"And?" he asked, "And what about Brownell?"

"He's an Okay kind of guy." She replied. "Sometimes I sit and chat with him if there's time. It's always small talk. I do know that there's lots of rumors that swirl around town about him. Some love him. Some hate him." She paused. "That's how it goes in life. That's how it goes when you've got a position like minister or judge, or political official."

"What kinds of rumors?" he asked.

"The usual." She replied. "You know. Rumors about his marriage. Rumors about sermons he's preached. Rumors about his political positions. There's even rumors about why he drives a red pickup and where it is seen."

"Where it is seen?" he asked

"Yes." She replied. "I've heard people say it has been seen in front of this house or that. You know how people are. He was probably just making a visit to a church member but people like to cook up things. There's even been rumors about his wife. Why she's so cold and uninterested in church but so political and gracious and smooth when it comes to social climbing."

"Interesting." Said Gunnerson.

"My break is almost over," said Addy. "Is there anything else I can help you with?"

"You've been very helpful," replied Gunnerson. "Here is my card. I'll be around town a few more days. There's more action here than in our town. If this Gregg fellow comes in again," he paused, "You would recognize him? If he comes in again, could you keep your ears open for any conversation you might hear? I'd appreciate it if you could give me a call. I'd love to come in and surprise him. At the least, he's in violation of his house arrest. On a hunch, we might discover a murderer."

Addy wasn't sure who he meant but she was game for some excitement in her job. The mysterious truck they had hauled off was the most exciting thing that had happened at DD in Loganwood in some time. Officer Gunnerson provided her with much to think about. Her imagination began to run wild.

"Murder!" she whispered as she leaned across the table so that only he could hear. "Murder." She whispered again thinking that she had just gotten an inside track on some of the rumors that might be more than rumor. They might be true.

CHAPTER THIRTY TWO

THE RUMOR MILL

No sooner had the fellowship time for Patchy's funeral broken up and the dishes washed and stowed, the phones started ringing.

There always was a good system of "you tell someone and you tell someone" in Loganwood. In the congregations of the town, the rumor mill was most effective. It didn't take long for news to get around.

Rev. Brownell was aware of the system. He had found it more effective in getting information out than if he broadcast it on the local radio station. So when Patchy had been found dead and it was time to tell the congregation, he didn't bother to print anything in a newsletter, bulletin or email. He just called one of four people in the congregation he knew would take the news and run with it.

Emma, Wilma and Thelma and Hilda had a regular coffee klatch going for years. Hilda and Thelma were next door neighbors on one of the side streets. Emma and Wilma were neighbors several streets over. They regularly met at Hilda's house in the mornings to express their concerns about anything and everything. Usually it was about church. And usually, their concerns was nothing more than gossip.

If they weren't complaining about Otty, the organist, it was the minister, or Patchy, or someone else in the congregation.

The concerns usually were things like; "He plays to loud." "I didn't like that hymn." "Who picks those hymns?" "He had some nerve mentioning so and so in his sermon."

"That sermon was exactly what Patchy, or someone else needed to hear."

This was all done, as each would admit, in the name of Christianity, kindness and concern. The truth of the matter is, it was all done to make themselves feel better because not one of them could find anything good about themselves. So, to trash others seemed to make them feel better about themselves.

Rev. Brownell knew this. He also knew that to get the information out that Patchy had been found, all he had to do was call one of the klatch members. He did. Within minutes the message was on its way. They had no clue that he was using them for his own devices and desires.

Brownell also had no clue that while they were transmitting his message, they were also including with it their own complaints and concerns about him. He was rather naïve upon occasion.

"No one," he often thought, "would guess what he was up to. After all, he was THE REV. LEE BROWNELL, a college graduate. Anyone else, especially church members, knew nothing and were beneath him.

So along with the news of Patchy's death, provided to the klatch by The Rev. Brownell himself, went accusations and assumptions about him and others.

The four planted the idea throughout the congregation and town, even before the news hit the papers of a murder, that Patchy's death might be a murder. It was a cruel thing to do to Patchy. It was even a crueler thing to do to the congregation. They had no proof but that didn't stop them. Little did they know that their rumor was on the verge of becoming true?

There is often a grain of truth in gossip. The little group used to joke about it. "We don't repeat gossip." They'd say amongst themselves. "No siree. We don't repeat gossip so you'd better get it the first time."

The congregation and town "got it" the first time. People were already on edge when the announcement, "Woman's Death Ruled a Homicide" hit the papers. For once the Coffee Klatch had gotten it right.

It was only the beginning of the end.

CHAPTER THIRTY THREE

COMPARING NOTES

"Thank you for taking the time to see me," said Officer Gunnerson. "I just came from Dunkin Donuts. It appears that things have changed quite a bit since we chatted last."

"For sure," replied Chief Blanc as she led him down to her office at the police station. "No doubt you've read the paper. We've gone from a simple accident to homicide."

"And we've gone from a woman burned up in Maine, to an abandoned truck." He replied.

"An abandoned truck?" she said with a quizzical look on her face. "What do you mean?"

"I took the opportunity to chat with Addy Teachout at DD earlier." He continued. "I was curious about a lot of things that have been happening here and in Maine. In particular, I'm not sure that Ophelia Pedens just happened to get burned up in our town."

"Really? What makes you think that?" she asked.

"Rev. Brownell and Ophelia were in Somewhere the same time." He answered.

"How do you know that?" She asked.

"From his red pickup truck and his number plate. I made a note of his license plate when he was up there." He continued.

"And?" she asked

"And RPMREV is licensed to The Rev. Lee Brownell. The very same man," he paused, "who just did Ophelia's funeral. Now he's done another funeral that is a murder here." He continued. "I spent quite some time with Addy at DD and she was a great wealth of information. She had no clue but I did."

"Information? About murder?" she asked.

"Not exactly about murder," he continued, "but definitely involving murdered people, rumors, and strange bumps in the day and night here and there. She made it clear that there's lots of talk around this place about Brownell. He's both hated and liked. I guess that's quite normal for many persons in a position of authority. All a minister has to do is go out of their way with a family of a dying person and the minister can do no harm."

"That's true." Said Blanc. "I have heard that he has been very kind upon occasion with the dying or sick. But I have also heard the other side of it. Sometimes he can't be found. Sometimes he is just blunt. What else did you hear?"

"I asked her about a white truck I'd seen parked at DD." He continued. "She told me that it had been parked in the same spot for a while and finally they had it towed. It must be at the impound yard."

"Did she say who it belonged to?"

"She didn't' know," said Gunnerson. "She had noticed a young man in DD several mornings in a row. He was all alone. He seemed to sit and watch people coming and going. He was interested in something. She didn't know what."

"Do you think he has something to do with the truck?" asked the Chief.

"I do," replied Gunnerson. "I think it belongs to a man from Somewhere Maine. His name is Gregg Morrison. I visited him up home a couple of weeks ago. I wanted to find out if he knew anything about the man in the red pickup truck. He didn't know anything other than he had seen him at the pull off south of our town. Gregg is a perv."

"Great! Just great!" said the chief in a most unprofessional tone. She was however, talking to another officer so she could let her professional guard down. "Just what we need is another perv in our town. What's he doing here?"

"Well," continued Gunnerson. "I'm not sure yet if he's really here. I suspect he is up to no good. If he's here I think it is because when I visited him I told him the red pickup truck belonged to Rev. Brownell from Loganwood. I think he's on a hunt for some..." he paused," you know what."

"Ass!" said the Chief.

"You didn't hear it from me, but you got it right, I think." Said Gunnerson. "At least that's what I'm thinking. In addition to that, he's in violation of his probation."

"Probation?" asked the Chief.

"Yes, probation." Answered Gunnerson. "He was involved with two others in murdering a kindly old man in our church. They got life in prison. Gregg got a year house arrest and years of probation because he was involved but mainly on the fringe. The perv spent most of his time either naked up in the steeple of the church or at the pull off dressed in a red dress and red stilettos. It was at the pull off that I suspect he connected with Brownell. I don't' know if they ever had a skin to skin, face to face meeting. At the very least he saw Brownell."

The chief leaned back in her chair and looked at the ceiling as if there was a clue to be found there. "So we have quite a mess on our hands." She replied. "Or at least we have a tangled web of people who seem to have connections or that are working at having connections."

"Exactly." Replied Gunnerson. "I'm just a two-bit bumpkin police officer but I'm not so stupid as to miss that something is going on here. There appears to be a lot of double living happening."

"Ophelia away from Loganwood," the Chief mused. "Brownell up to no good here and there? Gregg on the fringe working at getting more involved one way or another. If

Gregg is in Loganwood and that is his truck, then he's in violation of his parole."

"Yes!" said Gunnerson. "So I'm not only here chasing after Brownell and what he was doing in our town, now it appears I'm in pursuit of Gregg in order to arrest him and slap him in jail for good. He's either up to no damn good or just out for a good time, thinking that he can connect with Brownell for a toot and use blackmail to get it. He saw Brownell at our pull off and I'm sure he'd like to use that to get into Brownell's pants."

"If that truck belongs to Gregg," she answered, "then we may have more than we bargained for on our hands. Where has he gone if he is in our town as you suspect and as Addy at DD seems to have corroborated?"

"And," he continued as he finished her thought. "Who killed your victim? Was our fire victim murdered? And who's next? I attended Ophelia Pedens funeral, Patchy Frost's funeral and worship in between. That church is a strange place. I've always wondered how ministers could be so stoic in the midst of grief."

"Probably a drink or two before hand," the chief commented. "Or an hour of meditation. I was at both funerals. I didn't see anything unusual other than Brownell seemed rather florid in his descriptions of both women. How well did he know them? How much of what he said was the truth? I always think that at funerals. Ministers make the dead look like saints rather than tell the truth."

"I thought the same but I had no way of knowing," replied Gunnerson.

"Did you go to worship the day we found Patchy Frost dead?" She asked

"Yes." He replied.

"Did you notice anything unusual?"

"Not really. Pretty tame worship service," he commented. Only unusual thing was that the organist announced the organ was broken and they'd sing with the piano that morning. That didn't mean anything to me."

"They didn't' use the organ because he and Brownell had found Patchy Frost dead in the organ chamber. She'd fallen into the organ pipes." Said the Chief.

"Good grief!" exclaimed Gunnerson. "That's how she died? How sick."

"She was hit over the head with something a few days before, fell into the pipes unconscious and died. Pretty ripe by the time I got there after church that morning."

"And," continued Gunnerson, "They just went on with the morning worship as if nothing had happened? The congregation sat there ignorant of the fact that there was a dead body right in their midst on the other side of the wall?"

"Exactly," continued the Chief. "And you didn't notice anything unusual?"

"Nope!" he answered. "Pretty dull Sunday worship. That's one of the reasons I keep my distance when it comes to churches."

"Understand." She replied. "So it looks like we have the possibility of a murder that looks like an accidental fire, a definite murder in church and.."

"And," he finished her sentence, "A missing person who may be missing or may be lurking in the woods somewhere looking for his next victim to exploit. You have my cell phone. I'll be in town a day or two longer. Maybe something will come to the surface and this all will become crystal clear."

"I'll be in touch," said the Chief as Gunnerson headed out to his car. He wasn't sure what to do from here on out. It appeared he had circumstantial evidence, if evidence at all. He did have his suspicions.

CHATPER THIRTY FOUR

IT COSTS TOO MUCH

The Worcester Organ Builder Consortium had been in business for about 25 years. It was a conglomeration of organ building companies which were on their last gasp. In order to stay in business and keep maintaining the many pipe organs in the area, they had banded together. It worked for a while, but now some years later, pipe organs were less in favor. Many electronic organ companies had taken the bulk of their business. Churches could no longer afford new pipe organs no less maintain the ones they had.

Otty had called them to come and appraise the situation of the damaged organ at First Church. They usually came about once a year for an expensive tuning. Now the organ needed more than tuning. Its very existence was in question. Its repair depended upon an insurance claim, the generosity of the congregation and the cost of the repair.

"What happened here?" said Ansel Brundage, the vice president of Worcester Organ.

"Murder" said Otty in a rather matter of fact way as if it was something that had happened all the time. He had gotten over the initial shock of seeing Patchy all purple and bloated. All that interested him now was to get the organ repaired and save his job. Without the organ, the church didn't much need an Eastman School of Music trained, professional organist. Veona Rotowitz or some Susie left foot could do the job of playing hymns. The congregation didn't care much about Bach Toccatas and Fugues and other esoteric music, the kind Otty loved to play.

"What?" said Ansel.

"Murder." Repeated Otty. "You heard me right. Murder."

Brundage looked over the situation. Most of the great division had been destroyed. "The main part of this instrument is toast," he said.

"I know that!" said Otty getting more irritated by the moment. "What's it going to cost?"

"We'll have to replace all the pipes." Said Brundage. "There isn't one here that can be saved. And as for the wind chest, it'll have to be dismantled, hauled out and rebuilt. I imagine there's guck all inside it." He shivered.

"Whatever." Said Otty. "What's it going to cost?"

"My guess it'll be about $40,000 to replace these pipes!" he offered. "And then there's no guarantee until we get started on the work."

Otty gasped. Pipe organs are expensive to buy. Pipe organs are expensive to maintain but they do last for centuries if cared for. "Most churches don't care for their instruments, no less care for their members," thought Otty. "Forty thousand dollars" he slowly repeated. "Thank you Patchy Frost."

"What?" said Brundage

"Thank you Patchy Frost and the person who murdered here." He explained. We have enough money problems around here without having to raise more. I guess this will let us know how much the congregation thinks of their beloved, historic organ and music. I'm sure insurance won't cover all that."

"Is it too much?" said Brundage.

Otty laughed. "Too Much! Anything is too much. We'll be in touch."

CHAPTER THIRTY FIVE

DINING OUT

Evan Jansink moved out of the house as soon as he had turned eighteen. His sister, Amelia, had done the same several years before. They loved their parents but couldn't stand the façade they put up for other people to see. Evan and Amelia knew their parents were fake to the letter. The coiffed hair, the sport car, the perfect home was all gained at the expense of others, including the expense of their children. Thus, when Evan and Amelia came of age, they moved out.

Although the Jansink family members were highly critical of each other and everyone else in between, there was still a love that bound them together and brought them together. There was a trust that existed. Even if one went astray they would still stick together and support one another.

It was no coincidence and not unusual that Evan Jansink took an evening out to dinner at the local Riverlook Diner to announce his secret to his parents and his sister. He also felt compelled to come clean because of a discovery he had made. He needed advice as to how to handle what he had found.

"I'm sure you know," said Evan, "that my preference, my identity revolves around men. I have no interest in women or dating women. I love men. I have always loved men."

Evan, Arick and Amelia sat in silence not knowing what to say at the moment. When they spoke, it was his mother who offered a palm branch.

"Evan," she said, "we have known for a long time. As a matter of fact your father and I have often said that you were the only person who didn't know. Parents know their children. You will always be our son. You can always come to us. I am glad that you have finally felt safe to speak to us."

"What's the big deal," said Amelia. "This is a different day and age. It's only those prejudiced church people who call themselves Christian who enjoy shunning people different than they are. I quit going to church long ago because of those attitudes."

"I agree with you, Ame," said Evan. "A lot of what goes on in church is hot air. I've thought for a long time that if church people would love everyone instead of shunning people they don't like or who are different than they are there would be a whole lot less problems. I think church people should take credit for all the deaths from AIDS that has happened over these years. If we didn't have to hide and sneak around and could love the persons we love without being chastised and criticized, there would be a lot less promiscuity and unsafe sex."

"Really?" Said Arick. "I've never thought of it that way. The church has been responsible for lots of evil through the centuries. I guess we can take the blame for some of it."

"You have no idea," continued Evan, "the secret lives that people lead for fear of being ostracized. That leads us to live dangerous lives. People die deaths in more ways than one because of the behavior of church people and the lack of love."

They sat in quiet for some time thinking about what Evan had to say. His self-revelation to them would have been sufficient for that dinner party but the additional comments he had made brought them up short. Each imagined what he was talking about. Each tried to understand how they might have been complicit with other church people in causing pain and death upon those who are not welcomed and loved.

"You have probably never noticed," said Evan, "but there are places in Loganwood where people go to satisfy their desires. The Blue Hills is one such place. There are woods and paths and secluded areas. You can see all sorts of activities going on in the dark. I've been to those kinds of places."

Arick was shocked. He had never considered his son capable of doing such a thing as sneaking around in the bushes looking for. He didn't even know what word to put in his thoughts to explain what his son was talking about.

"Today I was out on Ravine Road, by Stone River," said Evan. "Know where I mean?"

Each nodded that they knew the road and area.

"I was out there sneaking around when I knew I had to say something to you. I knew you would tell me what to do." He continued. "It was a nice day and there was no one there but me. So I leaned my bike up against a tree out of sight and walked toward the ravine. When I got to the edge of the ravine overlooking the river I looked down and then I saw it."

"Saw what?" said Amelia.

He leaned forward and spoke in a whisper. "I saw the body of a man face down on the edge of the river. He must have fallen into the ravine. I immediately thought suicide. But then again, maybe I found a murder victim."

"What did you do," said his mother Kallie.

"I ran to my bike and got out of there as quick as I could." Said Evan. "I didn't want to be caught. Maybe someone would blame me for murder or something."

"Did you tell anyone?" asked his father.

"Only you just now." Replied Evan. "I've been thinking about what to do. I needed to tell someone. I guess the police. They are going to want to know what I was doing out there. I'll have to tell them the truth, I suppose. I'm afraid. I don't want to get blamed for something I didn't do."

"Did anyone see you out there?" asked Kallie.

"I don't think so" replied Evan, "and that makes me even more nervous. I have no witnesses and I am the only witness to what I found. What shall I do?"

"Report it to the police!" said Arick. "I'll go with you as soon as we finish our dinner. You'll have to tell them what you've told us. I'm sure the chief will probably want to keep your information in confidence. She'll know what to do.

CHAPTER THIRTY SIX

THE RAVINE

"Officer Gunnerson," said Chief Blanc over the phone. "Did you check out the truck that was towed and impounded?"

"Yes." Said Gunnerson on the other end of the line.

"What did you find out?" asked the Chief.

"The truck," answered Gunnerson, "belongs to Gregg Morrison, the fellow I told you about from up home. The fellow who is supposed to be at home on house arrest. Why do you ask?"

"I just had a visit from a family in town, members of First Church. They had an interesting story to tell." She said. "I'd appreciate it if you could come over as soon as possible."

"I'll be right there." Said Gunnerson.

It didn't take him long to get over to the police station. He had been staying at the Palmer House on Main Street, the big Victorian hotel.

"What's up?" he said as he settled into the chair across the desk from the Chief.

"It's more like, "What's down in a ravine." She quipped. "Let's go out to my cruiser and we'll go take a look for ourselves."

Chief Blanc knew the place that Evan Jansink had described. Upon more than one occasion the police had been called out there to answer a report of some less than honorable activity going on. It was a drug hangout. It was a hangout for all sorts of activity that needed to be hidden or which didn't want to be seen in broad daylight.

"Where are we going?" asked Gunnerson.

"Ravine Road," replied the Chief. "It's only a couple of miles out of town up this dirt road."

They rode in silence and in anticipation of what they would find. The Chief pulled the cruiser in off the road. There were no other cars around. They were alone as they walked the path through the woods down to the edge of the ravine.

"Evan was right," she said.

"Who's Evan?" he asked

"The young man who came with his family to tell me about this spot." She answered.

"And what of this spot?" He asked as they stood there surveying the area.

"Down there." She pointed. "Just as he said. Down there."

Gunnerson squinted his eyes to see. Through the undergrowth and just at the edge of the river he could see a body.

"Suicide? Murder? Accident?" He said.

"Don't know," she replied. "But definitely dead. Anyone falling off the edge of this ravine into the river wouldn't survive. Is that your man who goes with the truck that was towed? If so, no wonder he didn't come back for the truck."

"I think so," said Gunnerson. "It certainly would explain the abandoned truck. And considering the shady activity that he was involved in up home at our pull off, this is the kind of place he'd frequent. Maybe he came out here, hooked up with someone and ended up dead. Wouldn't be the first time a person got caught with their pants down and ended up dead."

"Well everything right now," she continued, "is mere speculation. Without any witnesses, no telling if it's murder, suicide or an accident. I'd better get the EMT and Firefighters out here to pick up the debris! No rush. He's dead."

They walked the path back to the cruiser where Chief Blanc made a call to the authorities. At the same time she called for backup to come out. They weren't really needed but it's always good to have a witness to a scene such as this.

It was no time before the Ambulance and Fire Engine appeared. Quick behind them was a reporter from the Loganwood Gazette. News travels fast. Police radios are monitored by the local papers.

"No doubt, after this reporter talks to us," she said, "we'll see a headline in the morning paper."

BODY FOUND AT BOTTOM OF RAVINE
Police investigating possible homicide

CHAPTER THIRTY SEVEN

WHERE IS HE?

"Well here we are and there's no Rev. Brownell," said Dudley Nolan. The Staff-Parish Relations committee had gathered on short notice. After experiencing a murder in their church, witnessing two funerals and ending up with a destroyed pipe organ, they felt it was time to have a conversation with their pastor.

"Where is he?" said Kallie Jansink. "It's just like him to not show up. Where is he do you suppose? You did notify him of the meeting, didn't you?"

"Of course I did!" said Dudley. "This meeting is not in secret. It's going to be all out in the open. We're going to have a frank conversation with him. But if "frank" isn't here it'll be hard to do." He laughed.

The others didn't get it. Dudley could have a rather "punny" sense of humor sometimes. People either got what he was saying and groaned or totally missed the point. Sometimes they'd say "What?" and he'd repeat the pun.

"Frank," he repeated. "You know. Like honest. We need to have this honest conversation with our pastor but if he's not here, it'll be difficult. No "frank" conversation without him."

"Oh. I get it," said Mercy. "Frank. I knew someone once named Frank." She laughed her innocent laugh. She wasn't trying to make funny. She actually didn't get it. Her naiveté could be a benefit or a hindrance to her participation on the committee.

"We'll wait another ten minutes to see if he shows." Said Dudley. "If he's not here by then, I'm going to assume we're being stood up. We'll go ahead without him.

"I think there's no point in waiting," said Barbara Nolan. "We've given him more than the benefit of the doubt. It's time we got down to brass tacks."

"Brass tacks?" said Tom Dougal. "Are we going to reupholster something? Maybe we can finally get that pulpit chair back to its original condition."'

"Brass tacks." Repeated Mercy. "I used to work at the local furniture factory. We used lots of brass tacks. I have a supply that they gave me when the factory closed." She didn't get it.

Barbara gave a disgusted look that she mixed with her usual, "I'm grieving guilty and grieving attitude." Dudley tried to ignore the small talk but the group was as interested in that as they were in discussing the pastor situation. It's lots easier to deal with nothing than deal with something.

"Speaking of reupholstering that pulpit chair, our sanctuary is looking pretty shabby these days." Said Esther Howlane. "I sit there on Sunday morning and notice all the cracks in the plaster. There's a big water stain way up high. The sun has faded the red carpet in places. To top it all off some of the windows, especially our big Tiffany window is leaking air. I just about freeze in winter."

"It all takes money," said Arick Jansink. "Lots of money. And now we need ever more money that Patchy fell into that organ and ruined it. She started all this."

"Hardly," replied Dudley. "Whoever murdered her started this."

"And who might that be?" Kallie said. "I bet someone right in our congregation did that. Who else would know she would be in that organ chamber? Who else would care?"

"I think we should paint the sanctuary dark lavender," offered Mercy, "and get some bright red carpet. I like purple."

"That makes me want to gag," said Kallie. "That's an old lady color and you're an old lady. I think it ought to be painted beige. While we're at it, we ought to get rid of those tacky pew cushions. And we ought to put a halt to this crazy rearranging of the altar Sunday after Sunday. And while I'm at it, I think we should just forget fixing the organ. That damn organist of ours plays too loud, too fast, and too weird. Organs are out, in my opinion."

"People, people," pleaded Dudley, "let's get ourselves under control. We spend way too much time with meaningless small talk and not enough time on why we are here."

"We're here because HE'S NOT HERE!" shouted Barbara.

"Who's not here?" said Mercy.

"THE PASTOR, YOU NUMB NUT!" shouted Barbara at Mercy. "THE PASTOR. THAT'S WHY WE ARE HERE."

Mercy scrunched herself down into a ball, making herself smaller than small. She was already tiny. She tried to disappear into the fabric of the chair.

Calista had been gently observing this mayhem that was escalating. "Now, Now, she said in her usual gentle tone. "We must be about peace. We must be about Jesus. After all that's why we are here. Love has brought us together."

"Bah!" blurted out Arick. "Love hasn't brought us here. Our Pastor who isn't here has brought us here."

"That's not true," said Calista. She rarely raised her voice. In fact in situations such as this she lowered her voice so that the others had to lean in to hear what she had to say. She always had something important to say. She continued. "We are here because we care about our church. We are also here because we got sloppy in our caring. We could have, should have had conversation with each other and our pastor long before we got to this point. I wonder now," she said, "if we can get this church back on a Jesus-like mission. I wonder."

They sat in silence for a moment. No one spoke. Some looked at the floor. Barbara's anger and grief bubbled over into her scowl. Dudley pondered how to gather this group back together.

"I think," He said, "that before we say any more, we take five minutes to sit in silence. It is good to sit silently. Eyes closed. Listening to the rhythm of our presence. Listening. I'll set the timer on my phone so we'll know when to break silence. Agreed?"

There was a little grumbling but each knew that if they were going to be able to speak openly and kindly about their concerns, Dudley was right. Dudley looked at each one seated around the circle and got acknowledgement.

"Good. The time starts now."

As silence descended upon the room and each one began to quiet, the breathing calmed and a rhythm settled in. Dudley knew, even though he could be all about business, that there is something to be said about people sitting in quiet or eating together. A oneness starts to happen that rarely occurs when there is just small talk and chaos. Sometimes the Spirit even descends upon one or all in the group and a Word comes that enlightens and empowers.

"The Lord be with you," said Dudley when the gentle timer bell dinged. "And also with you," they repeated. He continued.

"Let us pray. *Gracious God. We are gathered here with heavy and confused hearts. Evil has come into the presence of our church building and congregation. We have lost our way. Forgive us the devices and desires of our hearts. Forgive us when we have left undone the things we ought to have done. Forgive us when we have not loved as you love us. Forgive us when we have failed to love our neighbor. We grieve for our current lot in life that we have had a part in creating. We grieve for our pastor. Open us up to your kind spirit that we might, in honesty and love confront, encourage, empower, renew all that is and that can be. Thank you. In the name of Jesus Christ who has called us together. Amen.*

One by one, they came back into the present. If there had been a fly on the wall, even the fly would have noticed that the demeanor of the gathering had changed. Each still had their own unique personality and agenda to contend with but there was now more chance that the issues at hand could be discussed in a more orderly and kind manner.

"Thank you, Dudley," said Calista. "One of the things that is missing in our congregation is prayer. Maybe if we took more time together and alone in prayer, we would hear what we are to be and do."

"I like prayer," said Mercy.

"Thank you, Dudley," agreed Esther. "As the lay leader of our congregation, I will try harder to lead by example instead of by agenda and issues."

Barbara and Kallie, ever ready to pounce, didn't look too happy at the turn of the mood of the meeting, but they knew that they would get more of what they wanted if they complied with the way the meeting was going.

"Now," said Dudley. "As I see it, we have at least three issues to discuss. I'm disappointed that our Pastor is not here. We are at a point in our congregational life, however, that we must continue this meeting, if only to clarify the issues. We'll keep excellent notes of this meeting. In fact, if no one minds, I'll tape the meeting from this point on. And I'll meet with the pastor tomorrow. There's no point in beating him down any more than he's already been beaten down these past few weeks. Let's proceed with some kind of Christian charity." He turned to Esther. "Esther. You're the lay leader. Will you meet with me and the pastor when I fill him in on our meeting tonight?

"Yes. I'd be happy to go with you to represent our people and this committee." She replied.

"Good. Everyone agreed?" he asked. "Then let's continue. Here's what I see our agenda to be for the rest of this meeting. I suggest we spend no more than an hour so that we can all be home by 9 pm. I'd like to at least see the end of the football game."

No one had to say anything. Dudley knew that most people had a regular evening routine. If it wasn't a TV show it was a set time for bed.

"Good." He continued. "So here's what I think we need to discuss." As president of the Loganwood Trust, Dudley had experience with agendas and keeping meetings on track. He handed out an agenda upon which were printed three items. He had prioritized them in order of importance. The agenda was:

Prayer

Mismanagement or abuse of members

Financial Irresponsibility

Lack of Accountability

Prayer

"We've said the prayer," he continued, "so let us proceed. And while I'm at it, let us agree that not one of us will hold the group hostage or monopolize the discussion. "Mismanagement or abuse of members." It is my thought that one of the reasons we are losing people is that our Pastor is not paying attention to encouraging and caring for our members. I call it mismanagement. It might even border on abuse of members. It is also causing the people who are left to give up or just be apathetic saying "what's the use?" What are your thoughts?

"I agree," said Barbara. "I have heard people say that when they call in the middle of the night with some life or death crisis, he often says that he will be there in the morning. His response to need isn't very immediate."

"On the other side of it," said Calista, "I have known occasions where he has driven hundreds of miles to be at the bedside of someone dying. He would leave a meeting to be with someone."

"If he can be found." Snarled Kallie.

"Please, please," said Dudley, to Kallie. "Let's keep emotion out of our comments. So we have situations where he is or isn't present. He is not always responsive to the needs of others. Sometimes we can't find him, like this evening. Right?"

"I know I'm an employee, secretary of our church, but I'm also a member," said Marsha. "I have noticed and experienced a lack of compassion and kindness. Sometimes he can be very controlling. He doesn't always allow persons to use their gifts where they are needed. I've even heard him berate members for their doing something in a way that he wouldn't have done. He can be blunt and controlling. That stifles members."

"He was always moving the flowers on the altar," said Mercy. "Patchy was always miffed over that."

Arick expressed concern over the pastor's lack of interest in youth. Tom agreed and noted that the men's group didn't get much encouragement. It appeared from the discussion that the pastor was only interested in his agenda and when he wanted something.

"Sometimes he asks the most infirm and elderly member to do something that is really what he ought to be doing." Said Esther.

Dudley spent a moment gathering together the various thoughts of the group into a concise summary with examples so that he could present them to Brownell.

"Now," he continued, "let us talk about "Financial Irresponsibility."

"I'll speak to that," said Arick Jansink. "Our books haven't been audited in five years. I am wondering where we really stand on paying our debts. Where we stand on money coming in. What we are spending our money on. I don't trust the finances of our church anymore."

"We are going to find out sooner or later," said Tom. "We now have an organ that we can't use. That will keep some people away from worship. And the cost of repairing it may put us more in debt."

"I think," said Barbara, "that we ought to be paying more attention to reaching out with our money in missions and needs of the community than constantly pouring it into office supplies, building maintenance, etc. We use reams and reams of paper. Our woman's society is all about reaching out. We give more to missions and the needy than we do as a congregation."

"And what was with this secret loan he got interest free." Said Arick. "I think he hit up one of the members for money and now we have to figure out somehow to pay it back."

"Okay," said Dudley. "We have financial irresponsibility problems. There appear to be no checks and balances. The pastor does as he wishes and controls the activity of our treasurer. This leads us into our last topic for discussion. "Accountability."

"The fact that he is not here tonight speaks loud and clear," said Kallie.

"Can you explain that?" asked Dudley.

"Sure." She replied. "He's not here. Where is he? What is he doing right now? When he goes away for a day or a week, we have no idea how to contact him. And when he is here, he just barrels ahead with whatever he thinks he should do or wants to do, like spending money on office supplies."

"So, it appears he is accountable to no one." said Dudley.

"I would hope that he's at least accountable to God," said Calista.

"I would add," said Marsha, "that his lack of accountability is partly our fault as well. We haven't always kept good channels of communication open. Instead of dealing with issues that we hear from the congregation, we, as well as he, have just let things slide. It's difficult to be honest and forthright with each other. I just hope we haven't let things go so long that we can't recover from our current state of discouragement and disrepair."

"Is there anything else?" asked Dudley.

"I think," said Calista, "In addition to our concerns about our pastor, we could be concerned about each other. Not only do we want to be cared for and care for each other, we also ought to care for our pastor. When was the last time any of us have told him something good about what he has done. If we don't encourage and inform, he's not going to bother to encourage and inform and be accountable."

"Excellent point," said Dudley. "Does anyone have anything else specific to say?"

"At the risk of this sounding like a gripe," spoke up Tom, "I would just comment that I think when Otty and Brownell let us worship knowing that Patchy lay dead on the other side of the organ case was a good example of poor judgment and insensitivity."

"I agree." Said Calista, "But remember, they had just discovered her body. They were probably shocked. They may have just kept quiet until after worship as a way of being kind to those who came expecting worship. None of us expected to be told of a murder, nor did they expect to find a murder. So they went on with worship as if nothing had happened."

"I can understand that," replied Tom. "I still think it was a rather strange decision on their part."

In order to wrap up the meeting, Dudley chose to just make note of that and some final comments.

"We've reached the time for us to adjourn." Said Dudley. "I want to thank you all for your presence, your prayers and your concern. I think Esther and I will be able to meet with our pastor in an atmosphere that is less charged with emotion. Agreed Esther?"

"I know so," she said.

"I'll contact our pastor tomorrow morning and set up an appointment as soon as possible. In the meantime, "The Lord be with you." "And also with you," replied the group.

"Let us pray. Keep watch, dear Lord, with those who work, or watch, or weep this night, and give your angels charge over those who sleep. Tend the sick, Lord Christ; give rest to the weary, bless the dying, soothe the suffering, pity the afflicted, shield the joyous; and all for your love's sake. Amen."

"What a lovely prayer," said Calista. "Where did you get it?"

"It's from the Book of Common Prayer of the Episcopal Church." Replied Dudley. "It's one of my very favorites. The other prayer I use every night right before I fall to sleep is only two words. "Thank you." I think really it's all that is needed when we pray. "Thank you." I'll get you a copy of the other prayer. It's from the Office for Compline. In the meantime, let us pray my two word bedtime prayer.

"Thank You." All said.

"Thank you." Answered Dudley. "May you have a peaceful and thankful night?"

CHAPTER THIRTY EIGHT

SOMEBODY'S KNOCKIN AT YOUR DOOR

Marsha swung open the big front door of the church. "May I help you?" she asked.

"Is the pastor in?" replied Officer Gunnerson. "I'm from Somewhere Maine. I'd like to speak with him."

"Yes," she replied. "Follow me. I'm Marsha Hargrove. Been secretary here through many pastors. You can call me Marsha." She led him through the sanctuary with its Tiffany windows, two balconies and imposing pipe organ across the front. "We have three Tiffany windows, she said.

"Yes, I see." Said Gunnerson. "It is easy to tell a Tiffany window from others. Their colors are so brilliant. They must be worth a lot of money."

"They are," she replied. "Our pastor wants to sell one to raise money for some cause. The big window is the most prominent one. It is lit up at night. People don't often notice the other two because they are kind of hidden."

"Where are the other two?" He asked as if he had never been in the sanctuary before.

"They are up there," she pointed, "Hidden under the top balcony. It's kind of a dumb place for them. No one will ever miss them."

"Ah, I see," he replied as he craned his neck to see. He didn't let on that he had already been in the sanctuary several times. He'd never been noticed as an unusual visitor because he was always dressed in civilian clothes. For this visit he had donned his Somewhere Maine Officer's uniform. It made him stand out from the local police and the natives.

"And the pipe organ," she continued, "It was built by a local family that used to have the largest pipe organ company in the world. Their defunct now. But it can still be repaired.

It's not in working order right now. We had an accident with it a couple of weeks ago."

Gunnerson wondered why she called it an accident. Maybe the thought of murder in the sanctuary and in the place of her employ was just too much for her to handle. Many people are that way. They have difficulty being honest. They have difficulty cutting to the chase. They have difficulty calling something what it is. Kind of like a mother calling her infant son's penis his tinky-winky. "It's no wonder our country is so screwed up," thought Gunnerson. "If people would just tell the truth we'd be a whole lot better off than having to go on these investigation trails."

"Here we are," said Marsha. "Let me tell Rev. Brownell that he has a visitor." She tapped on the pastor's door. Gunnerson could hear a faint "come in" from the other side. He waited.

Rev. Brownell came to the door and invited Officer Gunnerson to come in.

"Have a seat," pointing to a couch. Brownell sat on an overstuffed wing chair facing the couch. "How may I help you?"

"I'm from Somewhere Maine," said Gunnerson. "I thought you might be able to shed some light on a situation we've had occur in our town. Since I've been in Loganwood, since Ophelia Pedens funeral."

"Anything I can do to be helpful," said Brownell as he uncomfortably shifted in his chair. To hear Ophelia's name was like hearing fingernails on a chalk board. He didn't ever want to hear about her again. "What connection do you have to Loganwood?" he asked.

"You may have read that we had a murder in our little church. A man was found stabbed through the heart with the cross off the altar. It was a grizzly sight. He was essentially nailed to the floor with the cross. Ophelia Pedens found him."

"She did!" said Brownell. "How did that happen? What was she doing in your neck of the woods?"

"She was on holiday. I had many conversations with her about the murder scene before she burned up in a fire." Gunnerson said, as he carefully watched Brownell's body language.

"And what does that have to do with me?" Brownell cautiously asked.

"Your truck was seen in our town about the same time. It didn't mean anything to me at the time," continued Gunnerson, "but just in case it might be important, I jotted down your number plate for future reference. RPMREV right?" he repeated.

"Right!" said Brownell. "I thought it would be fun to have that number on a red pickup truck. As a way of saying that I'm not some old fuddy-duddy minister. I like to travel in the fast lane. But it has been a disadvantage. I've gotten one or two speeding tickets. The truck is red. Strike number one. The number plate says I speed. Strike number two. I do speed. Strike number three. You're ought. Ticket!" He laughed.

Gunnerson said, "Well, let's hope strike number three doesn't mean forever."

"Forever?" said Brownell.

"Forever!" he replied, "as in "In Prison forever."

Brownell said nothing. Gunnerson could see that sweat was beginning to bead up on his forehead.

"So Rev. Brownell," Gunnerson continued, Can you tell me how is it that you were in Somewhere the same time that Ophelia Pedens was there?"

"Just a coincidence, I suppose." Answered Brownell.

"A coincidence?" asked Gunnerson, "that you and she would end up in the middle of nowhere in Maine on the same weekend?

"I suppose a coincidence." Said Brownell.

"Did you see or talk to Ophelia when you were in Somewhere?" He asked.

"No," he answered. "I didn't see anyone I knew."

"Did you happen to know anyone in our town named Quentin Patel?" Asked Gunnerson.

Brownell hesitated before answering. He wondered what Gunnerson was getting at. Did he think that he had murdered Quentin? Should he tell him the truth or try to lie. He always said "the truth will set you free," so he thought he might as well tell the truth. Maybe that would end this visit that was turning into an interrogation.

"Yes," he answered. "I knew Quentin Patel. But you don't think I murdered him, do you?"

"No," said Gunnerson. "We caught the murderers."

"Who was it?" asked Brownell. He was curious because the murder ended his reason for ever going to Somewhere again.

"Two women and a man." He replied. "The two women got life in prison. The man got off with just a year house arrest and parole because he was just on the fringe of the murder. On top of it he was borderline imbecile. A strange duck who liked to hang out naked in the steeple and hide in the bushes at a pull off south of town." He watched Brownell's reaction.

Brownell shifted in his seat trying to find comfort that no longer existed. "Strange character I'd agree." He said.

"So what was your connection with Quentin Patel?" asked Gunnerson.

"To be honest, and let it stay in this room?" asked Brownell.

"Please."

"Sex"

"Sex?" asked Gunnerson

THERE'S A HEARSE IN MY PARKING SPACE

"Yes. Sex." Repeated Brownell. "It was Quentin's secret in your town, and it's my secret here. We had been meeting several times a year for.."

"Sex." Finished Gunnerson.

"Yes." Said Brownell. "But there's no reason to go there anymore. And this fellow you mentioned?"

"Gregg? Answered Gunnerson. "I visited him several weeks ago after I'd found out you owned the RPMREV number plate on the red pickup. I went to his home. He answered the door stark naked. That just corroborated what I thought of him. He's an imbecilic pervert. Anyway, I asked him about your pickup. He indicated he had seen you at the pull off. He'd also seen you walking up through the woods. So I guess that explains what you were doing in Somewhere. I still find it very odd that you and Ophelia were in the same town at the same time. Did you and Ophelia ever connect while there? Did she see you? Did you see her?"

It was time to lie. "Not that I know of" said Brownell. I don't think we were ever at the same place at the same time. Anyway, we wouldn't be expecting to see anyone we knew. Nope, didn't see her. Too bad she burned up in that fire. I officiated at her funeral."

"I know." Said Gunnerson. I was at her funeral. I was at worship the Sunday the murder of Ms. Frost was discovered here. I was at her funeral too. This church is starting to be known as the church with a hearse parked out front."

"Yeah," laughed Brownell. "Tell me about it. I'm about ready for this run of funerals to be over."

"Well you won't have to officiate at the third funeral." Said Gunnerson.

"What do you mean?" asked Brownell.

"When I visited Gregg up home, I mentioned Loganwood and your name. It appears that when he found out who you were, he jumped his house arrest and headed for Loganwod. He's been in town since Ophelia's funeral. The lady at the Dunkin Donuts remembers seeing him several mornings in a row. He disappeared and left his truck in their parking lot. It's been towed and impounded."

"And Gregg?" asked Brownell. "Where's he?"

"Dead! Found at the bottom of a ravine. Suicide? We don't know. Murder? Maybe. Accident while out cruising the local pull off? Could be?" answered Gunnerson.

"What's this got to do with me?" asked Brownell.

"I suspect that once he found out," answered Gunnerson, "that you were in Somewhere for less than honorable reasons, he thought he could come down here, maybe blackmail you and establish a sexual relationship."

"That's sick!" said Brownell.

"Yes," replied Gunnerson, "Just as sick as the murder of Ms. Frost in your pipe organ. Chief Blanc and I have been in conversation several times."

Brownell didn't respond. Instead he shifted again in the chair and sat thinking about the situation he was finding himself in.

"Did you meet Gregg at Dunkin Donuts or anywhere else in Loganwood?" Asked Gunnerson.

"No and if I did I wouldn't know him." Answered Brownell. "He can't prove anything," he thought as they sat there staring at each other.

"We're keeping the file open on Ophelia Peden." Said Gunnerson. "I'm not so sure the fire was an accident. And Chief Blanc is keeping the file open on Gregg. She's not so sure, nor am I, that his falling into that ravine was suicide. It could be murder."

Rev. Brownell said nothing. He remembered the feeling of shoving, the startled scream and the thwack as the body hit the rock sides of the ravine and then hit the water. It made him shudder. No one had seen him so. Or had someone?

Gunnerson broke the silence. "I'll be in town a few more days. If you think of anything, here's my card. Give me a call. It appears that for the time being, your little sexual forays to Maine are safe. But in this business one never knows when light will shine on the truth."

As far as Brownell was concerned, it was more than light that was beginning to shine on his life. He was beginning to feel the heat. "They can't prove anything" he thought.

"I' hope I've been of some help. I'm sorry you've had such a time in your little town. That kind of thing isn't supposed to happen in the beauty of nature and a classic New England village. But I guess it does. People are people wherever they are. They often live more than one life at the same time."

"This is true." Said Gunnerson as he rose to leave. "Thank you for your help."

Brownell stood in his now open door as he watched Gunnerson cross the outer office and leave the building.

"Well" said Brownell to Marsha, "That was an interesting visit." As he closed his office door and returned to writing his sermon for the coming Sunday.

CHAPTER THIRTY NINE

DEAR GOD

His sermon preparation had been interrupted. He began to pray.

Most merciful God, I confess that I have sinned against you in thought, word, and deed, by what I have done, and by what I have left undone. I have not loved you with my whole heart; I have not loved my neighbors as myself. I am truly sorry and I humbly repent. For the sake of your Son Jesus Christ, have mercy on me and forgive me; that I may delight in your will, and walk in your ways, to the glory of your Name. Amen.

It was a prayer that Brownell had often prayed. The congregation prayed it with him. This time, the prayer had become personal. He thought that by speaking these ancient words, he could erase that awful scream that he heard as Gregg bounced off the sides of the ravine. He believed that he had gotten away with murder but getting away with murder and knowing you have murdered someone are two different matters.

There is such a thing as murder that lurks in the heart and Brownell was finally experiencing the consequences of his devices and desires. If no one else knew it and he'd gotten away with murder, it didn't matter. He knew it. Often that is enough to convict a person of the sins of their ways.

He prayed the prayer a second time. This time he whispered it out loud. He needed to hear to do more than silently pray the words. He needed to hear them. He remembered once counselling a young man who felt he'd murdered his father by writing a letter designed to cause a heart attack. The young man always brought up the subject of confession. Finally he left First Church and joined the Catholic Church. Brownell knew why. The congregation blamed him for the young man leaving First Church. Brownell couldn't tell them the young man's story, but he knew the reason he went to the Catholic Church was so that he could receive forgiveness of sins from the Priest.

Rev. Brownell now found himself in the same situation. He needed to confess. He needed forgiveness. He repeated the age old prayer. He whispered.

Most merciful God, I confess that I have sinned against you in thought, word, and deed, by what I have done, and by what I have left undone. I have not loved you with my whole heart; I have not loved my neighbors as myself. I am truly sorry and I humbly repent. For the sake of your Son Jesus Christ, have mercy on me and forgive me; that I may delight in your will, and walk in your ways, to the glory of your Name. Amen.

Confession was good for his soul but the headlines persisted.

WOMAN BURNED UP IN FIRE

WOMAN'S DEATH RULED A HOMICIDE

MAN FOUND DEAD AT BOTTOM OF RAVINE

"They come in threes," he whispered to himself. "Only good thing is I won't have to do this third funeral. He's dead and he took my secret with him.

CHAPTER FORTY

DUDLEY, ESTHER AND BROWNELL

As planned at the Staff-Parish Meeting two days before, Dudley Nolan contacted Rev. Brownell and made arrangements to meet. Dudley had thought it best that they meet on neutral turf with less charged atmosphere around them so he made a reservation to meet at Del Rossinas Itallian Bistro. They had a small private dining room where they could meet and eat in private. He also thought it best that they hold their meeting over a meal. Dudley often said that "Enemies don't want to sit down and eat together. It's the one common thing human beings do and it lets walls come down." It seemed to him that a meal would be less threatening and a kindly thing to do. So they met at 7pm on Friday evening. All arrived on time.

Once the waiter had taken their orders and the food was delivered, Dudley asked that the door be closed and that they not be disturbed.

"Rev. Brownell," he began. "I'd like to offer a prayer over our dinner and our meeting. *Let us pray: Creator God, we come together as your children. Be with us as we discuss your leading and your church. Grace us with your presence. Let us offer kindness and love. Bless this food. May it nourish our souls as it nourishes our body. Amen."*

"We were disappointed and discouraged that you didn't make the meeting the other night. We considered not holding the meeting," said Dudley, "but you had been notified that we were going to meet, so we decided to go ahead. We didn't want to meet in secret."

"I understand," said Brownell with a bit of caution. After having met with Officer Gunnerson, any meeting to him seemed like an opportunity to be trapped in whatever it might be that would bring him down.

"Everyone was at the meeting." Continued Dudley. "We had a very good and frank discussion. It is obvious that the committee members are all concerned about our church. There are also many people in the congregation and Loganwood who are concerned. There are rumors going around."

"And rumors," said Esther, "always damage, whether they are true or not."

Rev. Brownell took a forkful of his pasta thinking that a mouthful of food might defuse the atmosphere that he felt was building.

"We took good notes of the meeting," said Dudley. "Here is a printout that Marsha typed up for us and you to have." As he handed him a copy. "You'll notice that we discussed three topics. Mismanagement of members; Financial Irresponsibility and Accountability. I'd like to start with accountability."

"Okay," said Brownell.

"It has come to our attention," continued Dudley, "That on numerous occasions you are away from the parish and no one seems to know where you are. I can understand the need for solitude or renewal, but in this kind of work, it is good that someone, if only your wife, knows your whereabouts. For instance, "Where were you the week that Ophelia Pedens died in that fire?"

"Away." Replied Brownell.

"Away where?" Countered Dudley.

"You were nowhere to be found," said Esther. "We needed you. You didn't show up until we had the funeral planned and almost done."

"I'm sorry." Said Brownell as he hung his head. "I should do better at communicating with at least my secretary, my wife and," he paused, "You, Dudley. You're the chair."

"I agree," said Dudley. "I had a chat with an Officer Gunnerson the other day and he indicates that you were in his town the same time Ophelia died." He carefully watched Brownell for any hint of guilt or truth.

Brownell put his fork down and began to fold his napkin as if he had finished eating or was going to leave. "Just a coincidence, I suppose," he answered.

"A coincidence?" said Dudley. "Well, God does move in a mysterious way. Let's leave it at that. Why did you let the congregation sit through a worship service while Patchy Frost was dead on the other side of the organ case?"

"I didn't want to disturb their sense of peace and worship," he replied.

"So you made as if nothing had happened and you went right on with the service?" said Esther.

"Yes. There was time after the service to deal with our discovery." Replied Brownell.

"You had plenty of time to call the police," said Dudley. "Instead you called Will Elwell to come with the hearse. We're getting a reputation for having a hearse parked in the parking spot out front! Seems to me the right thing to do would have been to be honest, call the police, inform the congregation and then adjust worship to suit the situation."

"Poor judgment, I guess," said Brownell.

"We need to set up a plan for accountability. Rather than our pastor just doing as he or she likes, we need to have a way of communicating better." Said Dudley.

"Maybe you could train my wife in the new system of communication." He injected what he thought was a bit of levity. "She seems more interested in the Colonial Dames of New England and her Garden Club friends than me or the church."

They ignored his quip but they made note of it. "Well let this meeting be the beginning of better communication and accountability," said Dudley. "I'd suggest that we start to have monthly staff-parish meetings and that for the next three meetings we deal with the three subjects we've discussed. We certainly can spend an entire meeting talking just about how you can be accountable to the congregation and how we can be accountable to you. Agreed?"

Brownell saw that he had no choice to agree so he said, "Agreed."

"From now on," said Dudley, "if you decide to go off for several days, at least give us some way of contacting you. I'd rather hear it from you than from a police officer from another town."

The meals were getting cold so each picked a little at their dinner. It gave a break from what was turning into an interrogation instead of just an informational meeting about the previous meeting.

Brownell had lost his appetite. When they began to talk about financial irresponsibility he began to feel the squeeze on what he could or could not do that cost money. They mentioned about how he had hit up church members for interest free loans and then did some fancy footwork to repay the loan. They didn't think he had taken any money but they made it clear that they felt he didn't protect their finances.

The most disturbing topic during the meal, other than Dudley's reference to his conversation with Officer Gunnerson, was the intimation that Brownell had willingly mismanaged membership. "Sometimes," said Dudley, "the way you deal with members is less than benevolent. You ask little old ladies to do work that you ought to be doing. You put them at risk of bodily injury. You ignore the youth. You occasionally curse at members when they don't do as you say. When they do what you ask and it doesn't meet your expectations, you take over and undo what they did, only to redo it to your liking. In other words, you could work on your people skills. Let people use their gifts to do their ministry."

Brownell acknowledge their concern and half-heartedly indicated that he would try to do better.

"What else did Officer Gunnerson say?" asked Brownell as cautiously as he could.

"Just that it was odd that you were there the same time they had a murder" continued Dudley, "and that Ophelia was also there. He also mentioned a young man named Gregg."

"I don't know anyone by the name of Gregg," said Brownell. "It's all a mystery to me."

"It is to us," said Esther. "We want the best for our church. We want you to give your best. We do want the best for you."

"And," said Dudley, "We'd like to stop having a hearse parking in front of our church. But of course, that is out of our control."

"That's funny," said Brownell. "But it's not funny."

"We'll plan then," said Dudley, "to have monthly staff-parish meetings. We'll have the next one in about a week and hope that nothing catastrophic happens between now and then. Okay?"

"Okay." Said Brownell"

"And at that meeting we'll work on the topic of accountability. Yours. Ours. The church's. Let us pray again over our food so that we can finish with some care for each other. *Creator God. We thank you for each other and those not present with us. Care for the dying. Care for the needy. Calm and comfort us as we feast on this food and in fellowship with each other. In your name. Amen.*

CHAPTER FORTY ONE

WORSHIP

Several Sundays, two funerals and newspaper headlines had passed since last the congregation at First Church was together. In the minds of everyone, their world had changed, at least for the moment, if not for good. Ophelia was dead and buried. Patchy Frost was dead and buried. Their pastor had come and gone and come. An out-of-towner from Maine had been found dead at the bottom of the ravine at Stone River. The organ still did not work. And from Rev. Brownell's perspective of things, his life was falling apart by the minute. He had been interviewed all too many times. There had been way too much innuendo to suit his taste.

Rev. Brownell was at a loss for words. He heard far too many words over the past week. If it wasn't a conversation with Gregg about his being in Somewhere Maine, it was an interrogation by Chief Blanc or Officer Gunnerson. The last straw was the meeting with Dudley and Esther over the Staff-Parish meeting.

He heard their concerns. He even agreed with some of their concerns. Communication with members was difficult. His marriage lacked everything but a warm body to come home to and even that was stale. The finances of the church were in a shambles, not all due to his fault. The changing times had brought about less young people, fewer in worship and older members dying off. He thought he had done his best to keep the ship afloat but now it was sinking fast and he was going down with it.

With all this on his mind it was another Sunday again. "I'm running out of words," he said to himself. "I'm definitely running out of patience. I think I've just about spent all my spiritual capital." He was near tears. He knew he could not let his march toward a complete burn-out show to the congregation. They needed him more than ever. He needed them more than ever. Neither knew.

Sunday morning came far too soon after the chaos of the past week with funerals and meetings and the like. He prepared himself to stand in front of the congregation, doing the best job he'd ever done without knowing what rumors might have been spreading throughout the congregation and town. He also anticipated that both Chief Blanc and Officer Gunnerson would be there with all of their suspicions to watch his performance and to listen to the congregation. He didn't need to worry about Gregg Morrison. They'd plucked him out of the ravine.

He decided to play it safe. He would go for the old standards that the people loved. No creative, fancy worship footwork this day. Just the old hum-drum, we've always done it this way worship.

Otty arrived an hour before worship as usual. Brownell had asked the secretary to leave the hymn selections in the bulletin blank so he could visit with Otty and pick some nice gentle hymns. She also left the prelude and postlude listings up for grabs. The rest was lined out as usual. Opening prayer. Psalm. Scripture readings. Solo by Veona Rotowitz. Sermon.

"Otty," said Brownell. "Is there any part of the organ that you can use, at least for special music to keep the congregation calm?"

"Yes," he replied. "I can use the stops on the swell and choir manuals. We can get by. I might even be able to use the organ to sing with. I pulled the Great wind chest out so it won't make noise."

"Perfect," said Brownell. "I want us to do our best to make the most beautiful worship possible so that our people will be thinking about God and not about the murders that have been happening. What hymns do you suggest that they love to sing?"

Otty thought for minute and suggested, "Blest be the tie that binds" for a closing hymn. "It is well with my soul" before the sermon. Mr. Spafford wrote that in the dead of night after he'd found his children were lost in a ship wreck. And how about for an opening, "O God Our Help In Ages past."

"Perfect," agreed Brownell. "And let's have Veona Rotowitz sing .."

"There is a fountain filled with blood," said Otty.

"That's not funny," objected Brownell. "It has to be something they like and which Veona can sing."

"How about "Be Still My Soul." Suggested Otty.

"Perfect again." Said Brownell. "Alright I think we are all set. Let's pray we get through today's service without any more upset."

"Agreed" said Otty as he headed for the organ console.

It was nearly time for worship. Mercedes Haggenmacher was at the door, her usual post. She always had a smile and something pleasant to say to everyone entering. She had folded the bulletins and was ready to greet people.

Kallie and Arick Jansink arrived early so that they could sit in their usual seat. They usually had an alternate agenda than just worship. Mercedes didn't know what to think when Kallie snatched the bulletin from her hand and started yelling.

"THERE'S A HEARSE IN MY PARKING SPACE." Kallie shouted at the top of her lungs. "What's a hearse doing parked where I park."

"I'm sorry," said Mercedes. "I have no idea. I only hand out bulletins."

Kallie stormed down the aisle and headed right for Rev. Brownell's office. She slammed the office door behind her so he would know a mad person was present.

"WHY IS THERE A HEARSE IN MY PARKING SPACE?" she yelled at Brownell.

"How should I know," he answered.

"YOU arranged for it to be parked there, didn't you?" she shouted.

"Why would you think that?" he answered.

"You did it! I know you did it." Shouted Kallie.

At this point, Rev. Brownell lost his cool. "I'M NOT IN CHARGE OF HEARSES OR PARKING SPACES," he yelled back.

"YOU DID THAT," She countered.

"You know what this is, Kallie?" he said.

"WHAT" she screamed.

"THIS IS BULLSHIT! BULLSHIT!" he yelled back

The retort stopped Kallie in her tracks for a moment, but not for long. She took a deep breath and said, "Would you say that to someone else?"

"Yes I would," he said. "Especially when it really is bullshit. THIS IS BULLSHIT."

With that Kallie saw that she was going to get nowhere. She backed out of the office all the time with Rev. Brownell walking toward her. She joined her husband in their usual pew. She mumbled anger under her breath as she told him what had just happened.

Rev. Brownell was shaken as well. "Why is there a hearse out front?" he asked himself as he went to look. As he stepped outside the front doors of the church, passing people who were coming in and who were also wondering about the hearse, he saw Will Elwell.

"Will," said Brownell. "What are you doing?"

"I decided to come to church," said Will, and this is the biggest space to park the hearse."

"Well, thanks a lot," said Brownell. "Just what we need is a hearse parked in front of the church on Sunday morning during worship. The town will think for sure that we are dying or at the very least that we are nuts. Well come on in. You've parked it there now and everyone's seen it so you might as well come in."

Elwell and Brownell walked up the steps together. It was now time to begin worship. Most of the congregation had arrived. Many were standing in small clumps discussing what, Brownell could just imagine. Some as usual were praying. Others were just watching and reading the bulletin.

An air of expectancy, dread and gloom all at once hung over those gathered. They knew now that there was no dead body behind the organ case like a Sunday before. But they could not be sure. It was becoming clear that they could not trust anyone. When it reaches the point that trust is betrayed by leaders, especially the pastor, it is difficult for a congregation to carry on. If a congregation does carry on rather than give up the ghost, it often carries on with many issues from codependence to faithlessness, to lack of trust.

The sounds of the organ came from the organ chamber. Many were surprised that it still worked. They were pleased. They were especially pleased that Otty played a medley of old familiar hymns. He could see from his organ rear view mirror that the congregation was smiling. Some were singing along.

Rev. Brownell stood up and offered an invocation prayer and a call to worship. They were the usual. *"This is the day the Lord has made, Let us rejoice and be glad in it."* He repeated. He'd spoken those words from heart all his ministry.

The congregation sang "O God Our help In Ages Past." The hymn was so familiar to them that they sang "lustily and with good courage" as John Wesley used to instruct the early Methodists. They sang like Methodists, even though they weren't Methodist. Veona Rotowitz sang "Be Still My soul," to the tune of Finlandia. Several in the congregation were from Finland. They just loved that tune. It was their Finnish national anthem. And to them, and most of the congregation, the words about "the Lord being on their side," were very comforting.

Rev. Brownell had chosen a reading from I John as his text for his message. It was one that he had memorized over the years and often fell back on.

"Beloved, let us love one another for love is of God and he who loves is born of God and knows God, for God is Love."

He didn't even have to open the Bible to read it. He also paraphrased for them his favorite verse of all time from the Gospel of John 15. He said. *"Jesus said, I no longer call you servants. I call you friends. Love one another."*

He paused for a moment and then began: *Lord, Open our hearts by the power of your Holy Spirit that the words I speak and the words we hear might be what you have to say to us today.*

My friends, we are gathered today as God's people in God's house. Since our last worship our worlds have been turned upside down. We sit in a place where evil has visited. Loved ones, sisters who have worshiped with us are gone. We are alone. But we are not alone.

There was a time when I wondered, "Where is God?" There was a time when I wondered why I was in this business of ministry. I felt so incapable. I felt so alone. I felt so helpless. I felt so ignorant. Then one day, someone asked me to read the passages I read to you earlier.

As I read, I sensed that my preaching that was always directed out to others, was being directed to me. I discovered love. I discovered that God loves me. One of our church members in a church class some years ago described it with these words. "God loves everyone but he loves ME more." The class knew what she was getting at. When you discover God loves you, it feels like you are the only one in the world loved by God.

That is a frightening and comforting thing. It comes with much responsibility. When we are loved, we are to love. I was reading a book once as I was on the way to the funeral of a friend when I asked myself, "Why does my friend love me so much?" I heard the answer, "Listen to Love. Listen to how much God loves you. God is love. Love one another."

So today, my friends, my message to you is that we all fall and fail. We all sin and end up in the gutter. We all are alone at times. We all feel rejected and set up for the worst to happen. But remember. When in your darkest hour, when the storms of life are raging, when evil happens such as happened in this sanctuary and this town, God is love. God loves you. God forgives us. God allows us to move on. For God is Love.

The congregation sat in stunned silence. They had never heard such a sermon preached before. They were inspired. They were confused. They were questioning what was happening to their pastor. They were anxious about the downward spiral they were experiencing as a church. What was this all about?

As Rev. Brownell sat down, he realized that he had just preached his last sermon and it was the sermon of a lifetime. No matter what would happen now or in the future, wherever he went, God would always be there and would always be love.

The rest of the service was rather subdued as everyone looked at each other, prayed or stared at the floor. The singing of the closing hymns brought tears to their eyes. There were so many missing from their fellowship because of the uproar over the past few weeks.

Rev. Brownell asked the congregation to form a circle around the sanctuary. He walked to the back of the aisle by the front door. As Otty played "Blest be the Tie that Binds," Brownell encouraged all to hold hands in a chain of fellowship. Tears streamed down the faces of all gathered there. As the strains of the music descended over them, Rev. Brownell spoke the words of benediction. It would be the last time he would ever speak those words.

May God the Eternal keep you in love with each other,
so that the peace of Christ may abide in your home.

Go to serve God and your neighbor in all that you do.

Bear witness to the love of God in this world,
so that those to whom love is a stranger
will find in you generous friends.

The grace of the Lord Jesus Christ,
and the love of God,
and the communion of the Holy Spirit
be with you all.

As the congregation filed out of the church and onto the street, each in their own way greeted Rev. Brownell. Their emotions ran the gamut from joy, appreciation to anger. As he looked into their eyes, he saw a reflection of himself. He hoped that they saw forgiveness. He hoped that he saw love. He hoped that they saw the heart of a broken man and that they were benevolent toward him.

CHAPTER FORTY TWO

THE LAST STRAW

As the last persons left the church Rev. Brownell closed the door and locked it. He stood alone in silence before the large Tiffany window of Jesus, the Good Shepherd and wondered if he would ever be in the arms of the Shepherd like that lost sheep. The sun shone through Jesus' face and warmed the weary creases in Rev. Brownell's face. He began to cry.

He slowly walked down the aisle one last time. He stood before the altar. He untied his robe, removed it and draped it over the brass cross on the altar. The rope that had kept him so bound around his waist for some many services he curled on the robe. First Church was at the brink of going out of existence. He was over the brink.

He removed his clergy collar and laid it next to the rope. He left his church keys. He placed the note he had prepared on the altar.

Stepping back, with tears streaming down his face, he took one last look over the congregation he had been called to serve and failed. *"Father forgive me, for I know not what I have done"* he whispered as he closed the door behind him, got into his red pickup truck and drove off. He disappeared without a trace.

THERE'S A HEARSE IN MY PARKING SPACE

EPILOG
TWO WEEKS LATER

EPILOG

Rev. Brownell had left without a trace. His note admitted to nothing other than he had "sinned and fallen short from God." Since his disappearance the hearse was often seen parked out in front of First Church. In had become a symbol. The church was dying. It was almost dead. Rev. Brownell was not the only one responsible for its lingering unto death. People had left in droves. People were dying. First Church was getting a reputation for being the church with a hearse parked out front.

Rev. Brownell left the church in chaos. The church and the town wondered. Where had he gone? Was he still alive? Would he ever try to be a minister somewhere else? Was he guilty of all this chaos and murders?

Eloise Choate Brownell immediately sought a divorce and a return to here Colonial Dames of New England name, Choate. She also changed churches. She walked across the street and joined First Pilgrim Church. She felt more comfortable there among the elite of the town. She even found some distant relatives who were also members of the Colonial Dames of New England. She turned her back on First Church for good, not to say that she was ever entwined with the people at First Church to begin with. If she had stayed she would have been a reminder of her husband and what once was. She was happy to move out of the rectory and none too soon. She made little attempt to find where her husband had vanished to.

Under the stress of being the lay leader of First Church Esther Howlane had a massive heart attack that rendered her on life support. She lingered for several days. Her family chose to pull the plug. She died a peaceful death. She was spared from the duty of leading a congregation without a pastor. The one good thing that had happened to her was that

Rev. Brownell had asked her to be the Lay Leader. For the first time in her life she felt she was worthy. She died happy.

The next time a hearse appeared in front of First Church was for Dudley Nolan. He finally got release from his dismal marriage and the grief of losing a daughter in a massive auto accident some years before. His fat got to him. He died while on a treadmill having a heart test. He just fell over. Even though it happened at the hospital, there was no reviving him. Fat won over health. It took an oversize casket to carry him to his grave. The hearse groaned under its weight. His wife Barbara barely noticed that he was dead and gone. She continued to stare at the memorial stained glass window, grieving over her own guilt and the loss of her daughter.

The Jansinks found that their aggressive behavior did them in. The congregation chose to shun them. They weren't shown the door but when they left many said, "Don't let the door hit you on the way out." They ended up in another church in town that they attempted to control. They had no inkling that they would need a church sooner than later since Arick was suffering from liver cancer. He took it in stride since he often said, "Most of the people in his family died young of cancer." A hearse was ready and waiting in his future. What goes around comes around. How you treat people often comes back to bite you and that was the case with Kallie and Arick. It is also true that no one gets out of the world without some trial and tribulation. Some just find it sooner than later in life.

Calista McCann continued to send her sunshine cards to anyone she could think of. She even carried on a mail correspondence with Rev. Brownell. She knew where he was but was discrete and would never tell. Calista rarely gave up on anyone. She suspected that he was responsible for at least one murder but no one could actually prove it. So, she gave him the benefit of the doubt. She figured if anyone needed a kind word, no matter what he had done, it was Rev. Brownell.

Mercedes (Mercy) Haggenmacher continued to fold bulletins and greet people as they came to worship. It was an easier task as the attendance had dropped to a very few. She continually put on a bright face and hoped that before she saw the end of her days, the church would somehow begin to rally and come back to life.

As for Barbara Nolan, she was glad to be rid of her fat husband. She was sick of him. Both he and the house were constant reminders that her daughter had been killed because she had let her go out and paint the town red with her teenage friends. Barbara immersed herself in anything she thought would revive the church. Unfortunately whatever she did was tainted with anger and grief so not many people paid attention to her. She filled the void left by Kallie, Arick and Patchy Frost.

Why didn't anyone report the inconsistencies that were being observed? Rumors are fuzzy. Humans often default to do nothing. It is difficult to conceive that someone in authority is doing what they are doing, or thought to be doing. There's always the fear of reprisals. One person may know or think they know something. Each person seems to know just a piece of the puzzle. Often it is not until persons start comparing notes that action is taken to rectify a situation.

As for the rest in the story, Officer Gunnerson made a final visit to Chief Blanc and headed back to Somewhere Maine. He had a lot of information to digest but nothing specific. He went home empty handed with no murder solved. Instead, he now had three murders to think about: Ophelia Pedens, Patchy Frost and Gregg Morrison. He was disappointed to discover that Gregg had been murdered in the Ravine. He was deprived of the opportunity to arrest him for jumping house arrest. He would have loved to slap him in jail and let his imbecilic ass rot forever.

Will Elwell was thrilled to have the extra business. It don't bother him that people were dropping like flies, murder or natural. He never told that Patchy Frost had spoken to him from the preparation table. He knew who murdered her but would never tell. It was a funeral director's secret and it would stay a secret.

Otty Bourne continued to play at First Church. He embarked on a fund raising to get the historic pipe organ repaired. The congregation grumbled some that the insurance pay off was not enough to cover the repairs. That was partly because Otty wanted to add extra pipes to the organ. Nevertheless, the few remaining congregants chipped in and began the arduous task of getting the instrument repaired.

Veona Rotowitz had sung her last solo at the last service Rev. Brownell officiated at. Otty made it clear to her that her singing days were long gone. She sang flat and with a vibrato that could compete with the rumble of any pipe organ. She wasn't very happy about being taken down a peg but she complied and never sang again.

Within a week of Rev. Brownell's disappearance, Tom Dougal and the men's group had the pastor's office cleared out, boxed up and in storage. They immediately painted over the hideous paint color in preparation for a new beginning. During their work days, they often talked about the good old days and wondered about what lay ahead for them. The church was teetering on the brink of extinction. It definitely had lost its mission and meaning. It had forgotten its roots and why it had come together as a church two hundred years before.

The Staff-Parish elected a new chairperson and contacted the denominational officials for guidance. An all-points bulletin was put out by the police department at the request of the Staff-Parish. It yielded no results. Rev. Brownell had vanished into thin air. He was gone and there was no turning back.

Sometimes there is truth in the saying "The bigger they are the harder they fall." That a church has grown from two or three gathered together into large numbers is no guarantee that calamity, meaningless, and death will not darken its doors. People seem to be inherently bent to go from excitement at new beginnings to complacency to apathy, to resignation. Sometimes death comes. Sometimes death just lingers around the edges while a few struggle and resist. Big Church does not mean alive church. Many people does not mean freedom from decline. One person is never responsible for the entire state of an organization. It takes "two to tango" as they say. It takes more than a minister who has lost his way and fallen into sin, to bring down a small or tall steeple church.

With Rev. Brownell and some other significant people out of the picture, the stage was set for a funeral or a new awakening. Only time would tell.

CHARACTER STUDIES

THERE'S A HEARSE IN MY PARKING SPACE

CHARACTER STUDIES

REV. BROWNELL -- usually referred to as Lee. Rev. Brownell is an Ivy League educated 40ish man who moved to the Boston area from the Metropolitan New York Area. In many ways he is confused and conflicted about his calling and his personal state of being. He is clear that he has been called into the ministry but unclear about what that calling is to involve nor how he is to live out his truth. He is searching for love and thinks that he finds it by being a pastor of a congregation. His home life is as barren as a desert. Occasionally he finds love in his marriage. Most often, however, sex in his marriage is just that, sex. It is hardly eros and rarely approaches philio. Lust is a word that is constantly on his mind with caring a second. He understands Agape, that special love that wants the best for the other person, but he is most often wanting that for himself at the expense of others.

Rev. Brownell's wife is one of those women who always wanted to marry a minister. As such, she has ulterior motives for remaining in the marriage. She at one and the same time feels free and trapped. When she does consent to sex, it is more out of scriptural duty than love. To think that her husband might leave the ministry is to think that she will lose her societal position in life.

Rev. Brownell has been living a double standard, sometimes a triple standard. He is good at what he does. Creativity is his forte. Even though he is quite an excellent pastor, he is more excellent in building and maintaining a wall that gives the impression that he believes what he is doing. But he lives secrets. His life is a secret. He preaches against abortion yet he has had no problem encouraging his wife to get one. He had done that before and he would do it again. He is against same-gender marriage and LGBT people participating in the church yet he has maintained a gay relationship on the side in every parish he has served. In fact, the reason he had been to Maine recently, was to follow through on a relationship he'd developed when he had served a little church there. He killed Ophelia because she discovered his little secret. He did her in to protect himself, and in some way to protect his parish. Pastors often do strange things to maintain their position of trust and authority while at the same time betraying that trust.

Rev. Brownell easily played to the right wing positions of the parishioners, or left wing for that matter, in order to get money out of them. He often said, "There's money in the ministry" and he proved it by taking advantage of elderly old ladies who he encouraged to include him and the church in their will.

He has never had any problem taking advantage of the guilt of parishioners who had come for counselling and who then found themselves beholden to the pastor, having told too much of their sins and lives. "Entice," "Cajole," and "Co-dependent" were words in Rev. Brownell's vocabulary.

In other words, Rev. Brownell's career is all about him and doing whatever it takes to maintain control.

ELOISE CHOATE BROWNELL – married Rev. Brownell because she always wanted to be the wife of a minister. She had no interest in a salaried career. She abhorred the idea of being "just" a housewife. To her, being the wife of a minister was a career above all careers. She could have immediate societal status in the community and find instant gratification in that position. Eloise had little or no interest in sex, especially sex with Rev. Brownell. While on the one hand she was interested in being the wife of a minister, she could not stomach the thought of sleeping with one. To her, sleeping with a minister was like sleeping with God. God would see everything she did or thought about doing. Eloise had lots of fantasies about sex but none of them involved God. In fact, if she ever did participate in sex, she made sure that she went to confession first to confess everything she was going to do with her sexual partner, be it Rev. Brownell or someone else, the organist, perhaps.

When she did have sex with her minister husband, she did it prone and lifeless, allowing the fantasy to play out unspoken in her head. Eloise was as devious and conflicted as her husband. The only reason she stayed with him was so as to avoid town gossip and to maintain her standing in society. No amount of money could convince her otherwise.

PATCHY FROST – often referred to as "Pat" or "Patch" is a 60ish woman of the congregation who has been a pillar for decades. She is rarely seen without a large red rose in her hair or on her dress. She reeks of too much perfume, possibly to cover up the fact that on the outside she is pleasant and endearing, on the inside she has a heart of stone that is only interested in what she can get out of others and how she can get her own way. To say that she epitomizes her name, Patchy Frost, is an understatement. She is frosty to the core.

Patchy has her hands into everything and knows everything. She tries to control the pastor, the choir, the congregation and everything in between. Through her sweetness she wedeled herself a position on the Staff-Parish Committee. Rev. Brownell thought she would be a good asset and supporter. He couldn't be more wrong. Patchy had an opinion about everything and everyone. Patchy wanted her own way. Patchy could be as belligerent as a cactus and as sweet as a peach. The scent of her perfume and the sight of her big red flower was a warning that there was something brewing. Occasionally it was something good but most often it was something to the bad. She was into everything and for nothing. Her faith, rather than making her whole, made her into a tyrant, in passive and aggressive ways.

OTTY BOURNE – Studied organ at Eastman School of Music with some of the greats of a by-gone era. Because he had attended such a prestigious school, he often dropped the names of the world famous teachers who taught him everything he knew about organ and church music. Unfortunately, Otty didn't learn much when it came to ethics and morality. He had no problem finding someone in or out of his choir to have an affair with. This he did even though he was legally married. But his marriage left something to be desired. His wife, Vida Hood, was more interested in playing her cello than playing with Otty. Thus, while Vida was off playing in the Loganwood Symphony, Otty was playing an instrument of his own.

VIDA HOOD – Studied cello at Eastman school of Music. She met Otty there. They fell in love, more appropriately, lust, and married. Vida was first chair of the cello section of the Loganwood Symphony. She also carried on a heavy schedule of teaching and one night gigs. When Otty could talk her into it, Vida played for worship at First Church. She had no interest in religion nor Otty. The marriage and the gigs were a matter of convenience and money. It was something to do when she didn't have the attention of some other person, male or female, or a gig for the money.

BARBARA NOLAN is a retired school teacher who leans more often than not toward depression and nervous exhaustion. She involves herself in lots of community endeavors at the expense of her family and marriage. She is second generation Ukrainian who suffers from the toils of being raised by a domineering mother who is still alive. Her mother is a silent and belligerent but sometimes benevolent presence in her children's background and around the church. Grandma Salenko came on the tail end of the great mass of immigration to the United States. She brought with her all of her old world baggage that never quite fit in to raising a child in the new world. Barbara Salenko Nolan suffers.

Worst of all, Barbara suffers from having lost a child to an auto accident and her husband to non-stop grief. She blames herself for her child's death. If she had been more motherly and protective, her daughter would not have been out painting the town red with friends. She blamed herself.

Most of Barbara's time in worship was spent staring at a memorial the family had purchased in their daughter's name. It didn't matter that 17 years had passed since her death, she lived as if it were yesterday. She treated everyone most of the time as if others ought to be doing something to alleviate her grief and repair her marriage.

DUDLEY NOLAN – Barbara's Husband, had grown up in Loganwood and made it good. He was as round as humpty-dumpty and struggled non-stop to keep from falling off the wall of grief and responsibility.

Dudley excelled in everything he did except dieting. He clawed his way up from living in the slums to living on Magnolia Street which is where all the elite people who had made it lived. Dudley was a respected member of the community and president of Loganwood National Bank. He served on boards of many institutions and town in the state. He was capable anything he tried, all except for his marriage. His marriage since his daughter's death, was in name only. Sex came to an end. While Barbara grieved openly and would swing from pleasantness to belligerence, Dudley maintained his cool and grieved silently. Occasionally his grief would come out. Dudley also knew everyone's financial business in town and occasionally he let slip a tidbit or two.

CALISTA MCCANN was in her 80's. She was the matronly member of the congregation who loved and cared for everyone. While Calista gave the impression that she was in her declining years, she was far from it. At the age of 80 she sky dived with her son. She always said that when she was 90, she would do it again.

Calista maintained an extensive correspondence with any and every one she met. She sent cards to the homebound, the sick and infirm, the missing, and the lost. She visited many people on a regular basis.

Calista rarely said a bad word about anyone. She was always ready to help and be wherever she was needed.

MERCEDES (MERCY) HAGGEMACHER – was a sweet little old lady about 5 feet tall with grey hair and glasses. She never went to a hairdresser so her hair was always in a slightly out-of-bed style. Mercy, as she liked to be called, was a little simple but had a wisdom that often comes with age and simplicity. She could also be very funny. On one occasion, the day after she had cataract surgery, she announced to the congregation that she could hear well. The congregation laughed and then hugged her. They understood. Mercy would never miss anything going on at church. Never married, she had worked her entire life on an assembly line. In old age, she worked for the Lord.

KALLIE AND ARICK JANSINK had been Catholics in a former "life." Their attraction to First Church of Loganwood was a feeling that here they could take charge. They made a good pair. Kallie was actively aggressive. Arick was passive aggressive. Each wanted their own way and was bound and determined to get it. They often butted heads with Rev. Brownell. By their clothes and cars they gave the impression they were better than everyone else. Their children could do no wrong. As long as their children lived at home they were the perfect clones of their parents. But wait until the children were out of the home and out from under the control of Kallie and Arick. In the case of Kallie and Arick, first impressions were not the true impressions. Each held menial jobs while trying to claw themselves up by what they owned and who they knew. It didn't work. Eventually they left First Church to find some other place where they could be belligerent and controlling. They had two children, Evan and Amelia, both who left home as soon as they could.

WILL ELWELL is the local funeral director who loves to drive around town in his 1958 Cadillac Hearse. He is always seen polishing the car. He just loves it when there's a funeral. Sometimes he brings it to church with him. He also has a macabre side to him. On more than one occasion he claims that corpses have spoken to him in the process of preparing them for viewing. He won't tell.

VEONA ROTOWITZ is a long time member of First Church. She has been the resident soloist for decades. She was always ready to jump in and provide special music for any occasion. The only problem was that she couldn't sing anymore. Her singing was like finger nails on a chalk board. Off key. No more high notes. The congregation doesn't have the gumption to tell her to retire nor does she have the wits to retire.

CHIEF JANE BLANC had clawed her way into the position of Chief in Loganwood. She was highly respected for being one of the first Lesbians to hold such a post in Massachusetts. It didn't matter. The issue rarely if ever came up. She was competent and moral to the letter.

OFFICER CHAPPY GUNNERSON is from Somewhere Maine where the murder of Ophelia and Quentin Patel occurred. That was his first experience with murder. He was learning as he investigated the situations. He was becoming quite a sleuth in solving crimes and Loganwood added to his experience.

GREGG MORRISON – The Imbecile from Somewhere in Maine. Although he was implicated in the murder of Quentin Patel somewhere in Maine, Gregg managed to get off by pleading innocent. The Jury found it humorous that he liked to hang out in the steeple and at the Pickle Park, but they found him innocent in that he neither understood nor cared what the others who pulled off the murder were doing. Gregg spent a few nights in Jail and was then left to his own undoing. He was finished yet in hanging around less than honorable people and adding his two cents to the deceitful deeds of others, he was ripe for some more devious deeds. He hadn't learned anything from his run in with the law. He was still interested in hanging out naked, especially in a situation where he might get caught. He regularly visited the town pull off dressed in his red dress and red stilettos. He was always on the prowl. He was borderline imbecilic from an abusive family.

MARSHA HARGRAVE – had been the secretary at the church through a number of pastors. She was honorable and honest to a point. There were, however, things she would never tell. She always knew where Pastor Brownell was. But she never told. She didn't tell, because it was always information that she could hold over his head when it came time to ask for a raise or time off for vacation or, as she put it, "Good behavior."

Marsha was the sweet and helpful person in the office who always had an ulterior motive for who she helped and why she helped them. She was an asset and a liability to the ministry of the congregation.

BOOKS IN THIS TRILOGY

CHURCH MURDER MYSTERIES

"A Soul to Die For"
Vol. I
2013

"There's a Hearse in My Parking Space"
Vol. II
2014

"Up From the Grave"
Vol. III
2015

All books can be ordered from the Author
by email him at
mysterywy@gmail.com
or through
Amazon.com
or
Createspace.com

OTHER BOOKS BY THE AUTHOR

Geshnozzletoff;
A Children's book about a pig
2011

All About Acts:
Devotionals on the entire book of Acts
2012

Spirit Thoughts;
Poems, Recipes and Spiritual writings
2012

Uncommon Thoughts:
Devotionals through the year
2012

Downeast-UpCountry:
A Place, A Family, A Time
The story of a family in New Brunswick Canada
2012

Downeast-UpCountry:
A Place, A Family, A time
Expanded and Corrected
The Story of a Family in New Brunswick Canada
2014

ABOUT THE AUTHOR

Thomas L. Shanklin is a retired United Methodist pastor. He has served churches in Kansas, New Jersey, Vermont, and New Hampshire. He holds a Bachelor of Science Degree in Business Administration and Marketing from Fairleigh Dickinson University. He holds a Master of Divinity and a Master of Sacred Theology Degree from Drew University, The Theological School. Both theological school degrees have an emphasis on Methodist History, Theology and Bible. He has done work toward a Ph.D. in Religion and Theology at Drew University, The Graduate School, having completed all course work and passed the German Reading Exam.

Shanklin has published in numerous publications including Methodist History; Thantos, a Journal on Death and Dying; The United Methodist Reporter; United Methodist Insight; The Circuit Rider; The United Methodist Interpreter; Popular Science, various other periodicals and newspapers.

Shanklin makes his residence in New Hampshire and Florida. His interests include reading, writing, music, theater, art, history, travel, organ, piano, oil painting and much more.

THE COVER PHOTOGRAPH of a 1958 Cadillac Hearse was taken by the author.

Acknowledgements

It is with a great sense of appreciation that many people have been of assistance in the writing of this work. My beloved friend and colleague, The Rev. Alice Hobbs, has been an enduring support. Before her passing, she read volume one of this trilogy and offered invaluable advice.

Bonnie Schmalle, my neighbor in Florida, and Rebecca O'Malley, a scientist, choir member and friend both offered much assistance and inspiration. Bonnie read the manuscripts of both books and made invaluable corrections and edits. Mary Sutherland, my neighbor in New Hampshire and a professional editor, encouraged me to keep writing.

I am indebted to all of those who have endured my enthusiasm and conversation around murder and the plot in these books. There were many but I specifically name, Frank, Tahna, Jim, and many others.

Finally, the title for this book came from a conversation told to me by Jim at my church. He heard an elderly church member one day complain that "there was a hearse in her parking space," when she arrived one weekday. Little did she know that her comment would become the title of a book?

THERE'S A HEARSE IN MY PARKING SPACE